Journey Home
A Cat's Tale

Russell H. Plante

Whimsical Publications, LLC

Florida

To purchase the authorized electronic edition of
Journey Home: A Cat's Tale, visit
www.whimsicalpublications.com

Photographic Image in Chapter 2 courtesy of Edward B. Hopkins.
Used with permission.

Excerpt from "The Shelter of Each Other," by Dr. Mary Pipher ©1996, 2008. All Rights Reserved. Used with permission.

Cover art by Shyanne England
Editing by Brieanna Robertson

ISBN-13: 978-1-940707-86-0

Published by
Whimsical Publications, LLC
Florida

The sight of her stillness caused me to stop abruptly. I watched my mother sitting there, next to the mirror, entranced by the prisms of reflected light, and with curiosity, I seized the moment to sit next to her, looking down at our reflections together. Those images of my mother and me, reflected by the separate pieces of the broken hand-mirror, provided an indelible snapshot in time that I'll always remember. It was a never-to-be-forgotten portrait of the two of us.

My trance of that image was suddenly interrupted when Henry scooped me up by the scruff of the neck. I hung there from his large hand, my front and hind legs dangling and kicking in mid-air, and I cried out with a miserable howl, not understanding what had just happened. Holding me with an outstretched arm, Henry hastily opened the front door and pitched me out onto the front lawn as he shouted, "You're just another mouth to feed, and that's the last mess you're gonna make in this house. Out you go! And don't come back!" Then he slammed the door shut.

Looking back at that moment, I realize that Henry just didn't care about anyone or anything. His thoughts were centered only upon himself and his desperate state of affairs. He was enveloped by his own frustrations with no thoughts about anyone or anything else and, in that moment, particularly me.

Everything happened so quickly that I was dazed and ached from the sudden impact of hitting the ground. I was on the front lawn, upside down, staring up at the branches of the large oak tree just outside the front door of the house. Chickadees flitted from one limb of the tree to another as I watched, slightly confused about my rapid expulsion to the outside. I was used to watching all kinds of birds flying from branch to branch in that tree, but only from the inside of the house, not the outside, and certainly not upside down.

The sky was a bright blue with whispers of clouds that caused the shadows of each branch to change from moment to moment, not unlike the day's sordid events. As I lay there looking up, I began to understand the reality of what had just happened. Although still slightly shaken, I up-righted and steadied myself, took my first few steps, and looked around to see what kind of world I had been so rudely and cruelly catapulted into.

I simply didn't know what I was supposed to do or where

I was supposed to go. I was suddenly homeless, losing everything familiar to me. I wandered around the front of the house trying to figure out what to do next. I had only been out of the house once before and that was because I wanted to be outside. My father wasn't there this time, and the choice was not mine. I had no fear of the unknown as long as my father had been with me. Besides, I was used to always having a litter box and food in my dish whenever I got hungry. Now I didn't have anything.

I walked around the perimeter of the house and discovered the small front lawn was unkempt with scattered leaves from the old oak tree. The lawn hadn't been mowed and was almost up to the height of my chest, making it difficult to find my way through the grass. It hadn't rained in over two weeks and the few flowers that remained in a once manicured flowerbed that lined the front of the house drooped from the lack of water. A narrow brick walkway curved outward from the front stairs of the house, stopping at the edge of the driveway. I paused to get a sense of direction and managed to wade through the high grass as I crossed the lawn, continued on to the walkway, and then on to the end of the uneven gravel driveway. I looked around, side to side, at this new, strange, and frightening world. Deep down, I knew I had to accept the fact that I was now on my own. I was sure that in Henry's state of mind, he would never allow me back into the house.

We all face the eventuality of being on our own, but that reality can be more difficult to accept if the choice is not yours. As I wandered aimlessly in the driveway from one side to the other, I reluctantly built up enough confidence to make the only decision I could make—to accept my inevitable circumstance. I had no other choice.

I looked back toward the house, and a glint of sunlight happened to catch my eye. Hues of blue and violet colors sparkled from the tiny stained glass kitten ornament that hung in the window. I saw my mother sitting in the windowsill in the reflected light looking out at me. Her head touched the cool glass, knowing there was nothing she could do. She was alone now. I could only hope that someone would take care of her, and I wondered if I would ever see her again.

Acknowledgements

I would like to thank Eleanor Krueger, Lois Higgins, Julie Urban, and Tim Urban who read early versions of my original manuscript and provided helpful suggestions, giving me thought for enhancing the story line. I would also like to thank my wife Kathy, who read, read, and re-read the three major revisions and changes over the last two years, provided suggestions, and helped me to ensure this story embraced the connections in life that relate to each one of us. Thanks are also extended for support from Janet Durbin, who once had a cat named 'Patches'. And lastly, I would like to thank Brieanna Robertson for her editing skills, Jessica Keiley for proofreading the manuscript, and Shyanne England for the final cover design. Their contributions to this story will help to preserve this Journey we all share...

Part I

Abandoned

Chapter 1

Reflections

It's freezing cold and the bitter wind precipitates a chill factor well below zero. My whiskers are like frozen icicles, plastered against my face. The stench of garbage lingers as it slowly climbs the high steel walls of the dumpster that encompasses me. Wet, heavy snow continues to fall from the roaring blizzard above, creating a white blanket that squeezes the warm air from my lungs as I lay here. It's difficult to breathe. The sharp, chiseled jaws of a trap are wrapped around my foot like a shark taking a first bite, ensuring its victim can't get away. I'm not going anywhere; I can't move. I'm too weak.

A deep voice from within my past whispers quietly to me—reminding me.

Survive.

I twist my head to look upward and watch the large snowflakes as they cascade from the night sky—relentless. The eerie light from the only street lamp at the end of the alley paints a ghostly reflection from each flake as they continue to fall. A mist-like fog envelops the frigid air and my lungs ache as they dispel the little warmth I have left.

The wind howls and screams its message. Give up.

Even though the pain is unbearable, I can't lose hope. I can't just leave everything behind. I mustn't quit. There are just too many questions about my life that I need to answer. I see images of an overgrown forest trail leading to an old neglected graveyard. What was my father trying to explain to me as we wandered among those stone tablets, hidden from the world? Why did he abandon me? What happened to my brother and sisters? Will I survive this darkness and ever find a new home? These questions race through my thoughts—so many—like the leaden snowflakes that fall unmercifully upon me.

We all face different hardships, and there are moments, through no fault of our own, when we can become outcasts or can suffer from a backlash of hurtful words—words that are anything but empty. It is from those experiences that all of us have a tale to tell about important periods of our lives. I realize profound changes, both good and bad, have occurred during my first two years. I've come to understand more about the sentient world around me and about who I am. I didn't choose this path for my life. It chose me.

There are times when we simply have no choice in the direction life takes us, but misfortune can sometimes offer new opportunities. I've learned to persevere and contemplate the unexpected. The wind roars above, and I shudder from the cold, wet snow. I think about the past. Hope, family, and friendships are just a few of the many intrinsic values that I appreciate and understand now.

It's ironic that we often breathe contempt toward the unfamiliar, and yet contradict ourselves when we relish anticipation of the unknown. The experiences I have encountered may not be so different from those that anyone could face at some point in their lives.

The storm's wrath continues to swallow the night, and I think about the events that have led me to this moment and the relevance of my journey. Interrupted memories fade in and out—reflections of my past. I am alone. I am freezing and in pain, and there is no one here to help. I see images of my father, old weathered stone markers, and gnarled trees captured by time in a forgotten orchard. I think about our conversation—a distant past—and try to stay awake and understand his message.

The wind howls, the air grows colder, and the unrelenting snow drifts and gathers around me. The rampant squalls obscure the feeble light like a thousand distant stars until there is nothing more to see. My eyes grow heavy. The night darkens. Despite the cold, the hunger, the pain, the desperation to stay awake, I dream.

Chapter 2

Awareness

Thinking back about the very beginning, I remember the first few hours of my life as I shivered from the cold—ah yes, the cold that I have come to dislike so much over time. The circumstances were quite different then, however, because I found the warm, wet tongue of my mother comforting as she cleaned my ears and face. I felt safe, sheltered from the world.

My eyes focused themselves from the darkness into the dim light, barely able to define the contours of my siblings. I stretched out my paws and groped the blackness, just able to touch my two sisters and my brother. Although I could only see the dark outlines of their bodies, I could feel their warmth next to me. Their cries were like my own—scared of the unknown. I guess we all fear what we don't know or understand.

I could smell the dampness of the cardboard box where we were born and could hear my mother's labored breathing while cleaning us and trying to keep us warm. Although there was little room for the five of us, being confined together like we were somehow helped to lessen my fear of a new world—perhaps you could call it safety in numbers. We were together, and I heard her for the first time, calling my name.

"Patches, wake up, get some nourishment, and then you can sleep." Those were the first words spoken to me by my mother. As I fought the loneliness for assuredness and looked up to face those words, the darkness revealed a large figure crouched over me repeating my name once again, but with a deeper, calming sound—almost a whisper that lingered beyond its shadow—the reassuring voice of my father.

How I understood what my mother said on that cold, first morning, I really don't know. It's not like I had to learn a new language. The understanding was just there, unlike trying to learn a different, new language when you're older. It was actually later when I found that trying to understand what people were saying to me was altogether a bit more difficult. Their language was a whole lot different from mine. It took me longer to learn their language, and there were times when I still didn't always understand.

It was late March when I was born. The cardboard box was cold from the surly chill of a concrete floor, and the old, torn dishtowel that lined the bottom of the box provided little warmth. We were in the basement of an old two-story house, and the stagnant air from the remnants of a cold winter that lingered into a late spring left a musty, stale smell. The Maine winter had been a brutal one that year with more winter storms, cold temperatures, and snow than usual in our little coastal town. But even though conditions were less than ideal, it was comforting to know that we were together—and the world was new.

It took me several days before I could see well enough to find out what my siblings actually looked like. My brother and one of my sisters were a tortoiseshell color, having black and dark brown colors. My other sister had the same typical calico colors of white, black, and caramel as my mother and looked like her, except for one ear that bent slightly forward at its very tip. We were all long-haired cats, but I was a completely different color than the others. I looked like my father, who was considered to be a Maine Coon cat, a very large fellow. I had long black fur, with a white mane on my chest, a white patch from my forehead down both sides of my nose, a white patch at the very tip of my fluffy tail, and four white paws. The patches on my back feet were the distinguishing features that separated my father and me from each other, and of course, my relatively small size in comparison. Unlike my father, however, I had black patches on my back feet, giving me the appearance that I was wearing white socks with holes in them. I think that's why my mother had easily chosen the name she had given me.

As kittens, in comparison to people, we age much quicker. One year of our lives is equivalent to about seven years of people's lives, and for the first few years it may be even a little more than that. So only after about my first four months, I was at an equivalent age to a person of about four or five years old, just about the age when I could really get into a lot of mischief.

The first two months went by quickly that first year, and by early spring, I had investigated just about every nook and cranny in every room of the house with my two sisters and brother. We were at a curious age at that time and wondered about how things worked. As such, we occasionally got into trouble. But who doesn't at that age?

There was more than one instance when I received irate shouts from Henry Sullivan for doing things I wasn't supposed to do. There were times when he didn't feed us for the day because we shredded paper towels in the kitchen or pulled the toilet paper off the roll in the bathroom and ran it down the long hallway on the second floor to the top of the staircase. We thought it was funny, but Henry didn't think so. It was even more fun if we could get the toilet paper to roll down the stairs and onto the first floor. To say the least, Henry didn't think that was funny either.

Henry's wife Joanne was more tolerant of our misgivings. Their three children, ages four, six, and eight, thought our antics were at least entertaining, but never dared to tell their father for fear of how he'd react. You could never tell what kind of mood he was in. Most of the time, he wasn't a bad father. It was only when he drank too much beer that he became mean and somewhat hard to appease. You could never do anything right when he started drinking too much.

Henry had a good job working for the town as a maintenance worker, and he was proficient in many capacities. Some of his jobs included repairing water lines, plowing and sanding roads, and repairing recycling facility equipment. When he didn't drink, he was a hard worker and was paid well for his services.

Joanne, on the other hand, didn't get paid money for all the things she did. She had the full-time job of raising their three children—a hard job with many household tasks. Her rewards were far greater than anyone could ever pay her, though. She had the difficult but ultimately rewarding job of raising a family, and most of the time she took care of us cats as well—especially if Henry forgot to feed us, or on purpose forgot to clean our litter boxes—a nasty job that no one really wanted.

Henry and Joanne Sullivan rented the old two-story house in which we lived. They weren't affluent by any means, but they paid their bills as they became due and were able to get by from paycheck to paycheck. They even managed to save a few dollars whenever they could with the idea that at some point in their lives, they might be able to afford to purchase their own house.

Unfortunately, the economy was doing poorly the year we were born, and the cost of everything seemed to eat away at what Henry and Joanne had for savings and for monthly income. I think it was a money issue that caused both Henry and Joanne to decide that five cats were just too many to feed. And so it was a sad day for me in early May, during the first spring of my life, when they made a reluctant decision to give my sisters and brother to three other families in a nearby town. Before doing so, however, Henry told the children they could keep just one kitten. Since I was the smallest in the litter, and I would like to think the cutest, the decision was to keep me. That left just the three us—my mother, my father, and me.

My mother was an indoors only cat. She never ventured outside, nor did Joanne want her to. But my father spent most of his time outdoors and wasn't around very much. He had been known to disappear for several days at a time—occasionally, even a week would go by before he'd return. Because of that, I have only a vague memory of seeing him on a daily basis. My father was a pretty smart cat—wise in years, and much older than my mother. I always looked forward to seeing him when he would occasionally come inside to eat with us and tell us what he had seen in the outside world.

After my brother and sisters were gone, the house was unusually quiet. I had lost my playmates, and antics like rolling toilet paper down the hallway just wasn't as much fun without the proper help. As a result of my less playful activities, I remember spending a lot of time sitting quietly next to the kitchen sink, looking out the small bay window toward the back of the house. I would patiently wait to catch a glimpse of my father as he'd walk down a well-worn pathway and through an old arbor that entered a nearby wood and quietly hoped he would soon return. Then, he would disappear beyond my view, always leaving me to wonder where he went and what he did the entire day all by himself.

The old arbor that separated my reality from the unknown was rickety in appearance with much of its wooden latticework broken from many winters of heavy snow. But it still managed to separate the back yard of the house from the large wooded area that abutted the property. Rose bushes and ivy climbed over the top, making the entrance to the woods look like a dark tunnel.

I am always intrigued by learning and by seeing something new. Yet, at the same time, to complicate mixed emotions, I get apprehensive and fear about not knowing where an unknown path will lead or what will happen next.

The opportunity to follow such an unknown path occurred early in the fall of that first year. It's an afternoon I'll always remember because it made a difference in how I thought about things. I was only about seven months old at the time and the leaves were starting to fall, particularly from the oak trees. I managed to escape to the outside through an open door one afternoon as Joanne was bringing in two bags of groceries. I had been looking out the kitchen window and had just seen my father outside the house in the garden pathway heading toward the woods. My desire to be outside with him and share my world with his overcame my fear of leaving the house. Without much thought or hesitation, I vaulted through a small opening just before the storm door had a chance to shut. I was so quick that Joanne didn't even see me escape.

With all the energy I could muster, I quickly caught up to my father and, slightly startled by my sudden appearance, he turned around to question my actions. "What do you think you're doing? How did you get out of the house? And where do you think you're going?" he asked all at once as he continued his stride, passed through the opening of the old arbor into the woods, and onto the narrow pathway darkened by overhanging leaves and tree branches.

"I'm taking a walk with you," I replied. I panted and

gasped for air as I continued to quicken my pace.

My father just smiled and purposely slowed his walk so I could keep up.

"Okay," was all he said. Then he paused for a moment and said he had to catch his own breath, but I knew he had done so just for me.

I think that was just about the best afternoon I ever had. He showed me several types of herbs that grew wild at the edge of the woods next to the flower garden and introduced me to the smell of lavender, thyme, and of course some catnip that Joanne had planted—perhaps my overall favorite. He also explained several varieties of trees, what acorns were, how the trees grew, and pointed out the importance of knowing compass directions so you could always find your way home.

"See the moss on that tree over there?" he asked. "It mostly grows on the north side of the tree, at least here in New England, because it grows better in shady, moist areas."

He showed me some of the berries that could be eaten, as well as a small deer mouse that he thought might make a good meal as it ran across our path. But that morsel of food didn't look that appetizing to me, and I told him that cat food from a can was more appealing. I still remember his laugh over my reaction to that little running morsel of food. Then he agreed that the canned cat food at our house was tastier and certainly a lot healthier to eat.

While we continued to follow the old pathway, we came to a small clearing, separated from the path by a low stone wall. Its sides were uneven and open gaps signified its deterioration over time as it traversed the woods. Three teenage boys stood in the clearing, making strange motions with their arms and legs. The redundancy of their precise movements lent a natural rhythm to the surroundings as they moved in unison together.

"What are they doing?" I asked, intrigued by their synchronized motion.

"It took me a while to figure that out myself," my father replied. "They've been doing this all summer long. I sit and watch them and listen to them talk about what they're doing and how to do it better. They're actually practicing a form of something called Tai Chi. I've heard them call it Wu Tai Chi. I guess it's practiced as a type of meditation because it uses slow, controlled movements. Practicing the form is supposed to help gain strength, balance, breathing, and mental sereni-ty. At least that's what I learned by listening to their conver-sations with one another."

I was astounded by my father's knowledge. "Who are they and where do they come from?" I asked.

My father smiled at my additional inquisitiveness. "Just three teenagers who live in the neighborhood. They call themselves the three J's. I'm not sure what that means, though."

We watched them for a while as they quietly created their own solitude. The silence was interrupted only when they ended one type of form and started a different one. That's when one of them spoke. "This shorter form is a piece of cake compared to the longer form we just did."

"What's he mean by 'a piece of cake'?" I asked. "I know what cake is and what they're doing certainly isn't it."

My father laughed at my remark and replied, "It's only a simple expression meaning that the shorter form is easier to do. I've heard them say things like that before when they were practicing different forms."

When one of them spotted us sitting on the old broken down rock wall that skirted and separated the path from the small clearing, they stopped and approached the two of us.

"How are you doing today?" one of them asked as he came over and patted my father on the head. "Who have you got here with you? He looks just like you, only a miniature." The other two boys laughed and, taking a small package from one of their backpacks, offered us something called po-tato chips. I had never seen that type of food before. Since my father chewed a few pieces, I tried them as well and found them to be quite tasty—crunchy too—similar to some of our dry cat food.

After sharing some of their snacks, the boys gathered up their jackets, jumped over the low wall, and waved farewell to us as they left the clearing. We watched them disappear as they returned to the old pathway, and with a nudge from my father, we continued in the opposite direction further into the woods.

The further we traveled, the less defined the trail became

as it narrowed and, in a short amount of time, it darkened as the trees became thick. They leaned over each other, and their overhanging limbs became more prevalent. Then, un-expectedly, the trees parted, revealing an old apple orchard and several rows of strange stone tablets. The orchard showed signs of neglect with many of the trees having gnarled, weather-beaten branches and trunks. Surprisingly, a few of the apple trees still bore fruit. Oak trees were also interspersed throughout the site, and one of them, in par-ticular, enveloped one of the stones as the tree had grown over time. It was a solemn and desolate view to behold.

"What is this place?" I asked.

"It's an old graveyard," my father replied. "It doesn't appear to be attended by anyone. When I venture this far, I often wander among these markers. I've noticed that, over the years, acorns from nearby oak trees have sprouted new growth, and birds have dropped apple seeds, resulting in this continuum of nature. This is where people were buried years ago upon their deaths. Those stones are markers of their existence and the time period of their lives. It's a shame, though. I've never seen anyone ever visit this place." He sighed as he spoke. "Most of them have probably been forgotten."

As we walked among the old stones, some cracked from weather and time, my father took the opportunity and moment of the day to explain to me his perception of the world and what it meant to him. I simply didn't understand his message, though—I was just too young to understand what he was trying to tell me about time and mortality.

We walked and talked a lot that afternoon, and we paused and rested at several spots along the way. He told me he was getting older and because my stride was so much shorter than his, he kept slowing his pace so I could keep up. It was only the late shadows of sunlight filtering through the trees that prompted our return to the house before darkness overtook the day.

We arrived back at the house late that afternoon just as the sun touched the horizon, but even though I was home before dark, my mother wasn't very happy that I had gotten out of the house. She forbade me to do it again. I was her only remaining child, and she didn't want anything to happen to me.

Snow came early in November that year. My father continued to wander outdoors even through the worst of snowstorms and continued to stay away for several days at a time. On one cold day in the month of January, he wandered out into the woods and didn't return home. A few days passed, then a few weeks, and still he didn't return. He had never been gone that long before. Perhaps Henry didn't realize my father had tried to get back into the house or perhaps my father had just decided to move on to a new adventure. I didn't know where he was and, even though I never saw him often, I missed him and kept watching for him at the bay window in the kitchen. My mother missed him too. There were only the two of us then, leaving my mother a single parent. I guess it made me a little bitter thinking he'd just leave us and never return, and I wondered if it was somehow my fault that he had left.

My family had dwindled in size over a period of only a few short months, or what you would consider a few short years in terms of your life. Drastic things can happen to anyone in a short period of time. The fullness of my life at so young an age had diminished with the loss of family members, and I worried about what might happen to us next. It wasn't long before I found out what that would be.

Chapter 3

Seasons Change

Winter and the barrage of snow that fell during those cold months made time seem like it had also frozen. It was sometimes lonely, but my mother and I were good company for each other. We even investigated the damp, cold basement together. That visit ended somewhat abruptly, however, after we encountered a large rat skulking around empty cardboard boxes. He was as large as I was. My mother told me to hold my ground. She told me that if I didn't bother him, he wouldn't bother me. Since there was no reason to have any sort of altercation, we parted on somewhat amicable terms, leaving one another alone. That incident ended my curiosity about the basement and its contents, however, and also ended any desire to confront any other rats.

The long gray days gave me plenty of time to think about things, find ways to entertain myself, and play with the children. We also watched old movies together, anything from old black and white films that were bang, bang, shoot 'em up gangster films to colorful animated ones with pirates or talking animals, at least until I'd fall asleep in front of the television. But seriously, who doesn't do that? We also read a lot of books together. I'd watch the oldest teach the other two how to read. They'd examine each letter to form a word and then learn to enunciate each word and understand its meaning. I enjoyed hearing the stories as they read to one another. I paid close attention to the combination of letters and the words they formed.

The stories kept the winter months from dragging. It just didn't seem fair that the previous seasons of summer and fall had seemed so brief in comparison to winter. But being a little older, I was more aware of my surroundings and the sense of time. I guess that happens as you age.

Birds visited our backyard during the winter months and were of particular interest as my mother explained the diverse characteristics of crows, red-tailed hawks, finches, nuthatches, and many others. I found the crows to be the most captivating of all. I liked to watch them as they chased the hawks away from the smaller birds and outmaneuvered them in flight.

It was the end of that first winter in my life and the beginning of spring when Henry lost his job. The economy was getting worse, and everything was costing more. Unfortunately, Henry happened to be one of those expenses that had to be cut by the town, and therefore, he became a casualty of bad economics. Like many other employers, the town had to perform the same number of tasks with fewer people in order to cut expenses and stay within their available budget. Since Henry had been the last person hired in the town's maintenance department, he was also the first one laid off from his job. That's just the way the hiring system worked.

After several months of considerably less income, living on modest amounts from unemployment checks, receiving no job offers, and exhausting what little savings they had, tempers flared over money problems. To make matters worse, there were additional unexpected expenses. The refrigerator broke down, the washing machine had to be repaired, and the starter motor on their car failed, all within the same month. Monthly overdue bills for heating oil during the winter and utilities such as electricity and phone were constant reminders of their poor financial situation. Money woes took a toll upon a once cohesive and loving family. There were simply more expenses than income, and they were in constant debt. Their increasing debt worsened throughout the remainder of the winter and carried over into the summer months. By the middle of summer, they could no longer afford to pay their rent.

Henry's drinking increased and, as a result, so did his violent mood swings and depression. No matter how hard

Joanne tried to help Henry, there was nothing she could do. The constant reminder of excessive debt and the arguments finally convinced Joanne she needed to take care of the children and leave Henry. So on one very sad mid-September afternoon, when Henry was in one of his not so pleasant moods, she left with the children to live with her parents, two states away with a promise to return if Henry would just try to get better. Henry's excessive drinking had made a bad situation worse, causing the family ties to unravel and to deteriorate. It was not a good environment for the children.

With Joanne's decision to leave, however, and with everything in turmoil, my mother and I were left behind. After Joanne and the children were gone, I wondered if things could get worse than they were. Summer had ended and another season of change was beginning with cooler days and the cold realization that winter would soon be approaching once again. The house became quiet and devoid of human warmth, and my mother and I could sense an impending change to our own lives as well.

The transformation from one season to another on the coast of Maine was an unavoidable reality, not unlike the changes in our own lives from time to time. I knew the falling leaves would soon pass just like those I had witnessed the previous year. It would leave emptiness to the naked trees and a feeling of solitude as clouds overwhelmed the sun. Perhaps this reality of change was prophetic—that on a September day, in the early fall, over a full year after I was born, the unexpected happened.

Chapter 4

Vagabond

I woke to the warmth of sunlight streaming through the large living room window and across my sleeping whiskers. I remember the start of that particular day in distinct detail, not so much because of how it began, but more because of how it ended. Yawning and stretching like any young curious cat would do, I quietly jumped up onto the high windowsill to look out at the bright reds and yellows of a changing world. Only four days had passed since Joanne and her children had left the house. Since that time, Henry had been in a foul mood, cursing everything about his life and stomping around the house complaining loudly with only us to hear him. He had continued to drink even after Joanne had left, which certainly didn't help him deal with his problems or restore the family he had lost.

After I heard Henry talking out loud to himself in the kitchen, I decided to check our food dish and jumped down from the windowsill to see if he had remembered to feed us. My mother was curled up beside the couch, sound asleep. I wandered into the kitchen and saw Henry sitting at the kitchen table. He was just staring out the bay window, looking out into the woods. There were several empty beer bottles on the table, including one half-empty.

I trotted up to his chair and then jumped up onto the table, accidentally knocking the unfinished bottle onto the floor. The sound of breaking glass shattered the silence of the room as the bottle broke into shards onto the hard tile. I think it was the sight of foaming beer covering the floor and the splattered mess it made along the bottom of the cabinets that stirred Henry's anger and frustration. As I scurried off the table, he leaped from his chair and chased me out of the kitchen, throwing dishes at me that had been left by the sink, as well as any other loose objects he could manage to grab. An old hand-mirror whizzed by my head, narrowly brushing my ear, and split into two sections as it crashed to the floor just ahead of my retreat. Panicked by Henry's outrage as he chased me into the living room, I ran from room to room trying to avoid him and hoping he would calm down. After more verbal outbursts, his rage finally subsided, and he returned to the kitchen. The house grew silent once again, and I cautiously peeked into the kitchen and found him once again sitting at the kitchen table and continuing his stare out the bay window.

I decided it was in my best interest to leave Henry alone. The house had turned quiet once again, and I walked hurriedly back into the living room. My mother was wide awake from the commotion. I found her looking down at the broken hand-mirror lying on the floor. Sunlight snuck into the room as it peeked over the top of a large oak tree in the front yard of the house. The distinctive beams of light found their way through the panes of the large living room window onto the old broken hand-mirror. A small stained glass ornament of a kitten, hanging from the window's latch, filtered a portion of the sunlight into blue and purple colors that permeated throughout the room and danced across the back wall. It was the reflection of sunlight from the broken pieces of the hand-mirror, however, that had caught my mother's attention, as well as mine.

The sight of her stillness caused me to stop abruptly. I watched my mother sitting there, next to the mirror, entranced by the prisms of reflected light, and with curiosity, I seized the moment to sit next to her, looking down at our reflections together. Those images of my mother and me, reflected by the separate pieces of the broken hand-mirror, provided an indelible snapshot in time that I'll always remember. It was a never-to-be-forgotten portrait of the two of us.

My trance of that image was suddenly interrupted when Henry scooped me up by the scruff of the neck. I hung there from his large hand, my front and hind legs dangling and kicking in mid-air, and I cried out with a miserable howl, not understanding what had just happened. Holding me with an outstretched arm, Henry hastily opened the front door and pitched me out onto the front lawn as he shouted, "You're just another mouth to feed, and that's the last mess you're gonna make in this house. Out you go! And don't come back!" Then he slammed the door shut.

Looking back at that moment, I realize that Henry just didn't care about anyone or anything. His thoughts were centered only upon himself and his desperate state of affairs. He was enveloped by his own frustrations with no thoughts about anyone or anything else and, in that moment, particularly me.

Everything happened so quickly that I was dazed and ached from the sudden impact of hitting the ground. I was on the front lawn, upside down, staring up at the branches of the large oak tree just outside the front door of the house. Chickadees flitted from one limb of the tree to another as I watched, slightly confused about my rapid expulsion to the outside. I was used to watching all kinds of birds flying from branch to branch in that tree, but only from the inside of the house, not the outside, and certainly not upside down.

The sky was a bright blue with whispers of clouds that caused the shadows of each branch to change from moment to moment, not unlike the day's sordid events. As I lay there looking up, I began to understand the reality of what had just happened. Although still slightly shaken, I up-righted and steadied myself, took my first few steps, and looked around to see what kind of world I had been so rudely and cruelly catapulted into.

I simply didn't know what I was supposed to do or where I was supposed to go. I was suddenly homeless, losing everything familiar to me. I wandered around the front of the house trying to figure out what to do next. I had only been out of the house once before and that was because I wanted to be outside. My father wasn't there this time, and the choice was not mine. I had no fear of the unknown as long as my father had been with me. Besides, I was used to always having a litter box and food in my dish whenever I got hungry. Now I didn't have anything.

I walked around the perimeter of the house and discovered the small front lawn was unkempt with scattered leaves from the old oak tree. The lawn hadn't been mowed and was almost up to the height of my chest, making it difficult to find my way through the grass. It hadn't rained in over two weeks and the few flowers that remained in a once manicured flowerbed that lined the front of the house drooped from the lack of water. A narrow brick walkway curved outward from the front stairs of the house, stopping at the edge of the driveway. I paused to get a sense of direction and managed to wade through the high grass as I crossed the lawn, continued on to the walkway, and then on to the end of the uneven gravel driveway. I looked around, side to side, at this new, strange, and frightening world. Deep down, I knew I had to accept the fact that I was now on my own. I was sure that in Henry's state of mind, he would never allow me back into the house.

We all face the eventuality of being on our own, but that reality can be more difficult to accept if the choice is not yours. As I wandered aimlessly in the driveway from one side to the other, I reluctantly built up enough confidence to make the only decision I could make—to accept my inevitable circumstance. I had no other choice.

I looked back toward the house, and a glint of sunlight happened to catch my eye. Hues of blue and violet colors sparkled from the tiny stained glass kitten ornament that hung in the window. I saw my mother sitting in the windowsill in the reflected light looking out at me. Her head touched the cool glass, knowing there was nothing she could do. She was alone now. I could only hope that someone would take care of her, and I wondered if I would ever see her again.

What actually was the start of a normal day did not end that way. It was a new chapter in my life, with new lessons to be self-taught from new experiences, some cruel and harsh like a winter storm, and some uplifting like a warm spring day. You just never know what life will bring.

Looking back over my shoulder, I heaved a long, sorrowful sigh as I slowly walked out onto the paved street and into the surrounding neighborhood, leaving my mother, my home, and my old life behind. I was leaving a life I knew and was going to a life I knew nothing about. I wondered what my father would have done, and deep within me, I heard his answer—survive.

So at the equivalence of about a ten-year-old boy, my destiny was to become a vagabond, wandering from place to place and seeking food and shelter wherever I could find it. I looked back one more time to say goodbye to my mother. A tear slid from my eye as I turned away from her soulful look and took a first step into my new world.

Chapter 5

A Long Day

The pavement beneath my lightly padded feet felt warm as I took my first steps onto the nearby road and proceeded to wander from one block of houses to another. Buildings in the neighborhood appeared to be in a somewhat poorer section of the town and were in need of repair. Paint peeled from porches, steps were rotten, and roof shingles were missing on many of them. Several homes had windows that were cracked, and those beyond repair were boarded up, giving houses a battered look, beaten and unrecognizable from their former selves.

On some streets there were houses with front and back yards, not unlike the one where I had lived. On other streets, houses were packed so tightly together that you could almost reach out and touch the one next door. And instead of grass lawns, they had mostly areas of concrete and tar. By people standards, some were enclosed by waist-high, chain-link fences, many times higher than me. Gates separated the sidewalks from their entrances.

It was evident that I didn't know where I was going. I was terrified of everything that I saw and everything that was unfamiliar. Determined to cope with my fears, I continued my brisk walk through the neighborhood, looking from one side of the street to the other, gathering in the sights, the sounds, and the smells of my new outside world. I wandered up and down the narrow streets trying to figure out where I was going to sleep and how I was going to find food.

Those were my first thoughts—survival, a concept my father had tried to explain to me during our one outside adventure together. Thinking about my new situation, I realized that sometimes you don't appreciate what you have until it's gone. Then sometimes, it's too late to do anything about it.

There were sidewalks on each side of the street, and I chose to walk on the side that passed by several houses enclosed by chain-link fences. Since nothing could get in or out of the closed gates, I figured it would be the safest side of the street. Just as I got to the front of the first gate, however, a large dog ran toward me growling and barking. His sharp, pointed fangs were more intimidating than his size. Luckily, the dog was constrained by a leash so he couldn't quite reach the fence. Even if he had, the closed gate would have restrained him from reaching me. I had seen dogs in my own front yard, wandering around on their own, but I had never met one face-to-face or ever had one bark at me with such ferocity.

My verbal reply to the dog's surprisingly loud and deep growl was only one word—"Jeez." Not a particularly emphatic response. I was so startled by the unexpected act of aggression that I couldn't think of anything else to say at the time and almost stumbled off the edge of the sidewalk.

Recovering my balance, I turned to directly face the dog behind the fence.

"What's the matter with you? What's your problem?" I asked, somewhat befuddled as well as perturbed by the dog's reaction to my presence.

"I don't like cats," was the assertive reply.

"Listening to that unwelcome growl of yours, I can't imagine you would like anybody."

"You're new in the neighborhood, aren't you?" he said.

"Yeah, I guess you could say that. My name is Patches. What's yours?"

"My name is Carlo. Everyone knows who I am in this neighborhood, and now so do you. I'm just warning you to stay out of my yard. And one other thing—don't walk on this side of the street. I don't like anyone walking alongside my fence. You got that?"

"Yeah, you've made that perfectly clear. You could be a bit more civil about it, though," I replied, a little upset at the fact that I hadn't done anything to cause such a sarcastic exchange of words.

At that point, I decided it wasn't worth arguing any further with Carlo, who was many times larger than I was. Nor did I challenge his demand for me to walk on the opposite side of the street. As I mentioned, Carlo was a big dog, and there was no doubt in my mind that he meant what he said. He was part Pit Bull and part Boxer, and he had been trained to be mean and aggressive. It was obvious that his owner didn't want him having any good dog-to-human or dog-to-animal manners.

Unlike most dogs in the neighborhood, Carlo had a job that required him to have an aggressive behavior. He guarded a junkyard at night against trespassers. His owner also stored long strips of sheet metal in his own yard, so during the day, he was trained to chase anything that came within the confines of his owner's chain-link fence.

Without further discussion, I turned around, crossed the street, and continued my exploration of the neighborhood on the opposite sidewalk.

There were several brick multi-family tenement buildings across the street from Carlo. They lined the street in a long row and were so close to one another that you could open a window and talk to your neighbor across from you. The front of the buildings all looked the same, and many of the buildings had granite steps that led to small stoops as part of their front entrances. Their once distinguished brick façades were worn by wind-driven rain and snow of past winters. Porches were tiered on both sides of each building, one stacked above another, and clotheslines were strung on most. I could hear the pulleys squeaking as people hung their wash out to dry. I could also smell the decay of spoiling food left outside in garbage cans for several days. They were grouped together in front of each building, waiting for the town's trash collection truck. The sights, sounds, and smells of this new environment were overwhelming to my unaccustomed senses.

As I struggled to focus my thoughts, my attention was suddenly drawn to the clanging sound of bottles against the side of one of the metal garbage containers. Rummaging through the trash was an old man dressed in a dirty T-shirt, old blue jeans, and a tattered coat. He removed two empty bottles from one of the garbage cans, sat down on a bottom step in front of one of the buildings, and looked at his newly acquired possessions. Sitting there, I noticed his unlaced, decomposing shoes with no socks to cover his feet. The man looked lost, just like I felt, and I wondered whether or not he had a home.

I walked past the old man and continued down the length of sidewalk past the row of tenement buildings until I came to an old wooden fence that separated the multi-family dwellings from a different section of the neighborhood composed of single-story houses. As I came around the corner of the fence, I unexpectedly came nose to nose with another cat.

Somewhat startled by this brief encounter, the first words that came out of my mouth were, "Who are you?" I couldn't think of anything else to say. The other cat appeared surprised as well, but stood his ground as if anticipating some sort of reprisal to our sudden impasse.

Pausing for a brief moment, he calmly replied, "I'm Chester. I live over there in that green house with the white shutters. Where do you live? I haven't seen you around here before."

Having no contrived answer to his question, I replied, "I don't have a home."

"You're on your own?"

I hesitated for a moment, not sure of what to say, before replying, "Yes, I guess I am."

"Where do you eat and sleep?"

Despondent about my situation, I could only offer an honest reply. "I really don't know yet. I can't answer either one of those questions. This is the first day I've been on my own. The owner of the house where I used to live tossed me outside and said he didn't want me there anymore."

"That's harsh," Chester replied, and then proceeded to tell me about his own experience. I had never seen a cat like Chester before. He was a tan and gray tiger cat with a distinctive coat of stripes and swirling patterns and a thick furry tail. Like me, he had white socks on all four feet, but unlike me, he had no holes in them. I learned that he was seven years older than I was—that is in people years—and had been adopted by a family four years earlier. He had been on his own for two years before he was found as a stray and adopted.

Since Chester had a place to live, I asked him why he was wandering around outside on his own. He told me that the family who adopted him often let him run outside whenever he went to the door. He liked exploring the neighborhood. They didn't like letting him outside, but he noted that he could be very insistent and would cause a raucous by meowing loudly at the door until someone would finally grant his request. By being really obnoxious about it, he would often get his own way. He confessed to me, however, that he was smarter now than he used to be—you know, age begets wisdom.

The loss of his first home had been his own fault. He had previously lived in New York City and had sneaked outside from an apartment where he lived. He had gotten lost and confused, couldn't find his way home, and as a result, became a stray. To make matters worse, he had gotten trapped inside a moving van one night while seeking shelter, and was transported with some household goods to New England. Luckily, the family that moved from New York City found him in the large truck, sleeping on their couch, and adopted him. So he had learned two important things— always keep a sense of direction, and don't wander too far from home. He didn't want to be solely on his own again and was happy to be able to go to a home every night where there was plenty of food and a nice warm place to sleep, especially during the winter months.

Chester told me that he also had an adopted sister, Lilly, who was an indoor only cat. The family had adopted her from an animal shelter when she was only eight weeks old. She had never been outside on her own, and the family thought it best if she didn't wander the streets alone. She wasn't "street smart" like Chester.

Since Chester had been on his own at one time, he knew how to fend for himself. He knew how to find food and shelter. He knew a lot of things.

"I know what it's like not having a place to sleep or food to eat," said Chester. "I learned the hard way, on my own. If you'd like me to, I can show you around the neighborhood. I'm pretty familiar with it, and I can show you where to get a bite to eat and a place to sleep at night."

Considering my plight, I was relieved to hear those helpful words. Since I had started my journey that afternoon, finding food and shelter had been constantly on my mind. "I'd be really grateful for your help. This is all very new to me," I admitted.

Chester was happy to help. When he was in need, a family had adopted him and had given him a home. Now he had the opportunity to return an act of kindness by helping me. "Well, as far as finding food goes, there are a few small grocery markets in the area. Sometimes, the owners will throw some of the day old meats out by their truck delivery bays for stray animals. At least the food doesn't go to waste. If you meet up with any of the rats, though, you gotta be careful. If there's any shortage of food, they get pretty competitive and sometimes downright mean. Some of them are pretty big too, maybe not the size of some of those New York City subway rats that can get up to forty pounds or so, but at least as big as you are. There's also an old truck-stop diner called Gilligan's several streets from here. I'll show you where that is tomorrow. It's pretty easy to find. It's got a neon sign that always has at least one letter not lit, so it kinda stands out on its own. The food scraps aren't always the best in taste, but there's usually a lot of it. The owner's not a very good cook, but he serves large portions to his customers. Since not everyone finishes their meals at his restaurant, a lot of food gets wasted—especially the meatloaf. Even I won't eat his leftover meatloaf. Yuck!"

Chester continued to provide me with an abundance of useful information as he showed me around the neighborhood. He also apologized for not being able to take me home with him because he knew that the family he lived with couldn't feed any more animals. They already had two dogs and Lilly, plus five kids. So he didn't think it was wise to believe they could feed another mouth. His family just couldn't afford it.

As we walked through the center of the small town, Chester instinctively kept looking up at the sky to see if there was any possibility of a pending rain storm. He noticed the sun was setting low over the horizon with the persistence of a dark cloud covering. "I've got to get home soon. It's getting late. I'll show you a good place to sleep tonight before I leave," he announced.

"That sounds like a great idea," I replied, somewhat relieved to know that I'd have somewhere to go for the night.

Congress Street was the main road through the tiny business district and was just wide enough to allow parallel parking on both sides of the street. The variety of businesses was just enough to support the local neighborhood. Aging street lamps stood tall over the sidewalks that traversed both sides of the street, with their arched arms ready to provide a modicum of light when night arrived. Even this section of the town was reminiscent of aging structures in need of fresh paint and repair.

Chester continued his tour, pointing out some of the businesses he thought might be of interest and help to me. "There are two local restaurants on this side of the street within three blocks of the truck-stop diner that I'm going to show you later. One is a hamburger joint named Morty's Burgers, and the other one is called The Chicken Coop, and specializes in—you'll never guess—barbecue chicken wings. Sometimes there are leftovers at those places as well. First, though, we need to get you some shelter, especially if it decides to rain tonight. The clouds look pretty dark. I'll show you places where you can get some food and water tomorrow—that is, if I can get the family to let me out again in the morning."

There was very little traffic as we crossed Congress Street. Chester motioned to the buildings ahead of us and continued. "That's Luke's barber shop, the building that looks like it has a candy cane hanging outside. And next to Luke's is Hargrave's drug store. There are also two small retail clothing stores on this side of the street. One sells mostly men's clothing and is called Chandler's, and the other is Lemay's. They sell mostly women's clothes. Those two businesses are important because sometimes they throw out cardboard boxes from deliveries they receive and stack them in an alley in back of their stores. Some of those boxes make good shelters. I know that for a fact because that's what I once used when I was on my own in the city. I'll show you what I mean."

With that comment, Chester led me to the back of one of the retail clothing stores where deliveries were made. And just as he had predicted, there were several empty boxes stacked up against the back of the age-old brick wall. "You can sleep in one of those tonight. At least it will keep you out of the weather."

I eyed the stack of boxes. Some had been broken down flat and others had only been opened on one side and stacked one upon another like condominium apartments. "Thanks. I don't know what I would have done if you hadn't shown me around today."

Chester smiled, happy to think that he had been of assistance. "Don't mention it. I've been there, done that," he mused, stating an overused human expression. "I've got to go now, but I'll check on you again tomorrow, once I convince the folks to let me out of the house again."

I watched him walk away, thinking how thankful I was to have met him.

I had a lot to think about that first night of being alone and in a new and scary environment. As I settled down and tried to get comfortable inside one of the cardboard boxes, I thought about the life I'd had until just that very morning. A lot of life-changing things had happened in only a few short hours.

"It's been a long day, and I'm tired," I whispered out loud to the darkness. But there was no one to hear me. My thoughts were constantly interrupted by past memories, and I felt sad and wondered what would happen to me next. I buried my nose in my paws, hoping to hide from my despair, and wrapped my tail around my body for a little added warmth. I asked myself, What will I do tomorrow? and as I finally fell asleep, everything disappeared into an uncaring night.

Chapter 6

The Diner

"Hey, wake up sleepy head," was the sudden remark. It startled me from a fitful sleep. It was Chester. "It's time to get up and find you some food."

I smiled, happy to hear his voice, and replied, "I see they let you out this morning."

"Yep. I meowed until they just couldn't stand the sound anymore." Chester smiled as he started down the alley, looked back over his shoulder to see if I had gotten up, paused, and waited for me to catch up to him.

We left the alley and walked a few blocks past several of the stores he had shown me the previous day in the center of the town. We continued until we found ourselves in back of the truck-stop diner Chester had mentioned previously. The back entrance to the diner faced an enormous parking lot for semi-trailer trucks that exited the nearby highway. Wide alleyways on each side of the diner led from the back entrance to the front entrance of the diner facing the street. We walked around the building through one of the alleyways. The street in front of the diner was narrow and allowed only a few parking spaces. There were two long rows of windows that extended along the front of the building, and a double glass door served as the front entrance. The building looked like an extended double-wide mobile home with stainless steel panels. And sure enough, just as Chester had predicted earlier, there was a neon sign lit up with the letter "G" missing, so it read, "ILLIGAN'S".

"You know, that sign may be right for the first time," Chester announced, looking up at the sign. "If you eat too much of that food, you could be 'ILL-AGAIN'." He caught my faint smile from his attempt at humor. It was difficult not to find his comment somewhat humorous, and then on a more serious note, he said, "I'll show you where the cook throws out the leftover scraps of food." He then led me around the corner of the diner into the alleyway on the other side of the building. There was an old dumpster plonked next to the side entrance of the diner's kitchen that stood at least five feet off the ground. The green paint had faded and peeled over the years, exposing several rusted, jagged holes in the sides of the metal container.

"The cook throws all food wastes into that dumpster," Chester explained. "It contains leftover scraps of food from unfinished meals as well as raw pieces of meat, fat, and gristle, not usable. When the lid of the dumpster is open, you can jump up onto the edge and then down into the garbage. I call it dumpster diving. If the lid is closed, and you can't dive into the dumpster from above, you can still get inside by entering through one of those rusted holes. You need to be careful, though, not to get cut on the jagged edges when searching through the garbage for food. Sometimes it can get slippery in there, and you can slide into one of the sidewalls.

"The name of the man who owns the diner is Harvey Stunk. He's also the cook. Now, you might ask yourself, why would the diner be named 'Gilligan's' if the owner's name is Harvey Stunk? The answer to that question is provided by another question. Just ask yourself, would you want to name your diner, the 'Stunk' diner? So, Harvey just made up a name, one that would not be associated with the smell of cooking bad food." Chester was jubilant as I smiled once again at his continued attempt at some appreciated humor. I think he knew it helped to take my mind off my troubles.

Knowingly, Chester continued. "Harvey throws leftover scraps of food into this large dumpster every day." With those words just spoken, a slight breeze managed to waft its way down the alleyway toward us. Like a low ocean tide on a hot, muggy day, we could smell the leftover and spoiled food from the large container. The outside of the dumpster was filthy. You could easily tell that it hadn't been washed down in months. It smelled of rotting meat, even though it was emptied by a trash collection business twice a week.

A high-pitched squeak sounded as the screen door attached to the side entrance of the diner opened. It always squeaked. Today was no different. Harvey came out the side door with some partially eaten pork scraps for the trash, left over from unfinished meals. A cigarette butt dangled from his lower lip, and his extended beer belly was the first thing you noticed about him. His apron was filthy from food stains and his hairy arms and unshaven beard completed his unkempt appearance. If you knew that it was he who cooked the food, you would probably shudder at the very thought of eating anything at the diner.

"That's Harvey Stunk!" exclaimed Chester, excited that he could point out the person he had been talking about.

Harvey was a terrible cook. Worse yet, he didn't really care or even try to improve upon his cooking skills or, for that matter, even his appearance. The food selection on the diner's menu was simple, edible, inexpensive, and plentiful. That's what made the diner popular. It certainly wasn't Harvey and his unrefined ability to cook. The meals were what people in the neighborhood could afford and were used to eating. The diner had been there for years, and the menu seldom changed. Truckers ate there more for the convenience of accessibility from the highway and for the volume of food served rather than anything to do with flavor.

Harvey had a somewhat gruff look about him and a mean personality as well. He didn't like people who asked for handouts. There were always homeless people asking for free food, and he always turned them away. He had no sympathy for anyone, no matter what their situation was. He didn't like stray animals either. He always shooed them away. It was his nature. He had experienced a hard life growing up with a single mom and had left home at an early age to fend for himself. He and his mother never received any help, and he never understood or appreciated anything she ever tried to do for him. His attitude toward others was not a positive one, so he never helped other people, animals, or essentially even himself for that matter. He had worked long and hard as a short order cook in many clubs and small restaurants until he had saved enough money to start his own business. He had accomplished all of that on his own. That's the person he was.

Chester and I watched as Harvey opened up the heavy lid of the dumpster and tossed in the bag of half-cooked, uneaten pork scraps. "Some of those scraps of meat might not be bad," Chester remarked as he backed away from the diner's entrance so Harvey wouldn't see him. I followed Chester's example. Harvey didn't notice us and returned to the diner through the side screen door, forgetting to close the lid to the dumpster. The screen door squeaked once again as it slammed shut.

"Now's our chance," exclaimed Chester as he easily jumped up onto the edge of the dumpster. "Come on, just jump up here and then over the edge like this." He motioned, and I watched him disappear over the edge into the garbage below.

"Okay," I replied, not sure if Chester had even heard me. It looked like he had simply disappeared.

Following Chester's example, I jumped into the dumpster after him, and we both had our first meal together of leftovers from the previous night.

"Not bad, huh?" remarked Chester as he finished chewing his second piece of pork.

"Not bad at all," I replied, realizing that I had forgotten how hungry I was. I was famished and most anything I ate would have been considered a delicacy. I immersed myself into chewing and even gulping down pieces of pork fat imbedded in the meat. The scraps were cold and tough, but the flavor made up for the condition of the meat. I devoured what scraps there were and then thought I should have had something to drink next because my throat was extremely dry from swallowing so hard.

"Didn't you already have something to eat before you left this morning?" I asked.

"No, I skipped breakfast so I'd eat a meal with you this morning and keep you company," replied Chester.

Then, as promised from the day before, Chester showed me where I could get water to drink. "When it rains," Chester explained, "it's better not to drink water from puddles in the alleyway. Stagnant water in these dirty puddles can make you sick. I learned that the hard way when I lived alone in the city. Drink the water that accumulates in the shallow lids of the discarded, washed out food containers. The rain usually forces any stagnant water out of the lids so it's fresher water. When it doesn't rain, Harvey usually washes out the empty food containers with a hose so the smell doesn't get too bad in the alley. Even Harvey has his limitations on what smells bad. So either way, you should be able to get fresh water."

I was fortunate to have accidentally met Chester when I did on that first day of being homeless. Over the weeks that followed our first meeting, Chester taught me just about everything he could think of in order to help me survive and deal with my new environment. He taught me how to observe the things around me, how to fight if I needed to, how to understand myself better by putting myself in the place of others and treating them as I would want to be treated, and how to be a good and decent cat. He taught me how to make shelters from discarded materials in order to keep out of the weather, where to find food, what foods were safe to eat, and what foods might not agree with my stomach—like hot peppers from Harvey's "hotter" menu items. We talked a lot about Chester's own experiences as a stray with the hope I might better understand what I was facing. There were many times when we would simply lose track of time and chat until well past dark. But there were also times when we would just meet up, chase mice, explore, and play. We grew to be good friends, and I always looked forward to seeing him.

The rest of September went by quickly as I tried to adapt to my new surroundings. I often found food in the dumpster by Harvey's diner. It wasn't always tasty, but it was something to eat—better than starving, which wasn't an acceptable alternative. Rats ate there also, however. Chester had warned me about the rats. Many of them were much larger than I was, and they usually weren't very nice when it came to foraging for food and sharing anything edible. I tried to avoid being in the dumpster at the same time they were, but that didn't always happen. If a rat happened to be there at the same time, I avoided a confrontation by leaving the dumpster before I was noticed. Under conditions other than sharing food, the rats were otherwise friendly. They usually didn't bother me, and I didn't bother them. I always had a feeling, however, that eventually, one day, there would be an unavoidable encounter. It wasn't pleasant when that day finally came.

Chapter 7

Oh Rats!

My eventual encounter with rats happened unexpectedly on one particular day in October. I was at the corner of the alley next to the diner, searching for food, when Harvey opened the side door from the kitchen. I heard the familiar squeak of the screen door and scampered down the alley toward the dumpster, knowing that Harvey was probably throwing out some table scraps. I arrived just in time to see Harvey disappear back into the side entrance. I ran over to the side of the dumpster, thinking to myself that it was time to get something to eat. I was hungry.

The heavy lid of the dumpster was still open. As usual, Harvey had forgotten to close it. I was getting fairly adept at making it into the dumpster with one leap. Crouching down, I gathered my strength, and with one spring, I jumped up and over its edge into the garbage below. This time, however, instead of landing on a soft mess of food, I landed abruptly on top of a very large rat. Needless to say, he was extremely surprised. He was also very unhappy about the sudden impact to his body, as well as the somewhat unexpected and unasked for company.

The force of my jump flattened the rat so all four of his feet were spread apart. It looked as if a steamroller had just run over him—something that would be funny to anyone watching, as long as you didn't consider the possible consequences of such an act. Before he could recover, I quickly rolled off the somewhat flattened rat and found myself peering directly into two large ruby-colored eyes. His large brown face with long whiskers, small-defined ears, and thick silky hair was only inches from mine. Not only was I staring at one rat, but two others quickly approached from behind him—more gray in color than brown.

The rat I faced was still trying to catch his breath when I panicked at what I had done and exclaimed, "I'm sorry, I didn't mean to land right on top of you when I jumped in here. I was just trying to find something to eat."

"Not here you don't," was the quick reply from the large, perturbed, panting rat. His long, pointed whiskers flinched as he spoke. "You should watch where you're going."

"I said I was sorry and meant it. It's difficult to anticipate where I'm going to land when I jump over the side of this dumpster. Besides, I didn't even know you were in here. By the way, my name is Patches, and I am really sorry that I landed on you like I did."

"Forget about the so-called apology," replied the rat, still somewhat agitated from being crushed. "I'm Amos, and now that we know each other's names, it still don't make us friends. You jest ain't gonna eat here with us—that's all I need to say to you."

Feeling just a little irritated and upset at both his attitude and his demand, I had a lapse in my timidity and responded. "You know, you don't have to be such a glutton and eat all the food scraps yourself. You could share a little."

"I don't think so," replied the rat with a slightly mumbled slur to his voice. "There's enough here for jest the tree of us. That's how I see it. So git outta here and find yourself some food elsewhere. This is our food pantry."

"You sound like one of those 1930s mobsters I've heard in some old television movies," I replied, trying to change the direction and tone of the conversation. I was still trying to remain friendly and apologetic. That tact didn't work, however.

"I don't care what I sound like," was the response. "Jest git outta here. You've done enough damage for the day. I've got pieces of pork rinds stuffed up my nose thanks to you."

It was all I could do to keep myself from laughing at his remark. I got the point, however, that he was serious. I figured that Amos wasn't a bad rat, just a mean one when it came to sharing his food supply. He simply believed that what was his, was his, and what was someone else's, was his also. There are people like that as well, you know, ones who don't like to share. I thought Amos might feel differently about sharing if we got to know one another better.

Amos and the two rats behind him moved menacingly closer to me as we continued to discuss the food situation. "There's not enough food here for us all. We don't want you here." Amos was emphatic with his delivery of those words to me. He meant business and I knew it.

"That's a fact," responded the other two in unison. As I listened to their increasingly heated protests, I remembered words similar to those spoken by Henry on the day he threw me out of my home. I winced as I recounted those hurtful words and backed away from the rats and from the middle of the dumpster, still hungry.

After receiving many of life's lessons from Chester, I graduated to what you might consider as being "street smart." Being about sixteen months old, I was growing into a large cat, even with some days of going hungry. My chest of long, white fur was starting to resemble a lion's mane, making me look even bigger than I really was. I could defend myself if I had to, but I never started a fight. I preferred friendly solutions and found there was always more to gain than to lose by having a peaceful compromise instead of a physical altercation. The odds were against me in this situation, though, and I decided the smart thing to do was to leave the dumpster and forget about trying to get something to eat there. I was outnumbered, and thought I'd look somewhere else for food.

With that thought in mind, I leaped back up onto the edge of the dumpster and jumped down onto the pavement below. I hadn't had anything to eat all day, so I decided to continue my search for food.

Despondent, I visited a few houses in the area to see if I could get a handout. There was old Mrs. Wilkes who lived in one side of a white duplex on Pine Street. She lived alone with an older cat as her only companion, and the two of them were very happy together. If there was any cat food left over from feeding her own cat, she would often leave me whatever she could in a dish outside her front door. She could barely afford to feed the cat she had.

Unfortunately, she had no extra food for me that night. The dish by her front door was empty.

There was also Mr. Hoffstedder who lived two houses down from Mrs. Wilkes with his wife, Dora. They had a dog named Bracken, who was a friendly Corgi. He was different than other dogs I had seen in the neighborhood. He was real low to the ground with short legs and, for some odd reason, he had no tail like other dogs did. That dog would eat most anything, including vegetables, as well as other things I won't mention. But if Bracken didn't eat all his supper, which wasn't very often, they would put some of the leftover dog food out by the end of their walkway for me or any other stray animal that happened to be passing by so that we would have something to eat. Even though it was dog food, it was still nutritious—not great tasting, but still filling. They seemed always willing to help out in some way, and it was nice of them to care. There were a lot of older homes on that street with older residents, but most of them were not in the best of financial conditions, so they weren't able to provide food for stray animals. Not all days were therefore blessed with handouts, and I didn't find any food that night anywhere else. The rats had won that day, and I had lost.

Hoping I could get a bite to eat without any rats around to complicate matters, I waited several days before returning to the diner. When I arrived, Harvey Stunk happened to be in the alley by the kitchen's side entrance to the diner. As Harvey approached the screen door, he was surprised when a large rat ran by both of us into a nearby drainpipe that led to the diner's storage shed and then disappeared from sight. Harvey was visibly upset upon witnessing the fat, furry creature's disappearance into his shed. That's when he spied me sitting close to the screen door.

"I've seen you here before, scrounging around for food!" Harvey exclaimed out loud as he quickly walked over and snatched me up before I had a chance to avoid his advance. "It's time you earned the leftovers you eat here!" Harvey sneered as he spoke and held onto me with both hairy arms.

Trying to escape, I wrestled against his strong, hurtful grip, but I couldn't get free. I thought I was a goner.

Chapter 8

Pranksters

Harvey was well aware that rats lived in the storage shed attached to the diner. He had seen them on many occasions as they darted in and out from their hiding places. He just could never catch them. He had laid traps inside the shed and had caught a few of them once in a while, but the rats got smarter over time and learned to avoid them. Once they understood how the traps worked, Harvey never caught another one.

Rats could get inside the storage shed by using a drainpipe that extended underneath the floor of the shed and into the alleyway next to the dumpster. After a water pipe had burst in the kitchen, flooding the shed, Harvey had installed the drain. He figured if anything like that ever happened again, the stored food supplies wouldn't be spoiled from water damage. The one thing he didn't count on, however, was the fact that the drainpipe was a perfect transportation tunnel for the rats as a direct route from the alley to the shed. Chester would have said that they sort of had their own version of the Holland Tunnel—like the one that connects New York and New Jersey.

Although the shed didn't have its own heating system, enough warm air permeated through the wall from inside the diner and kept the room just above freezing temperatures in the winter. Harvey was therefore able to use the shed as a walk-in refrigerator in the winter months for extra food storage. In that way, he could save money by purchasing food in larger quantities from week to week. The only problem with having extra food reserves stored in the shed, however, was that rats would eat some of the food and cause spoilage before he had a chance to use it. That cost him money, and Harvey didn't like losing money, especially if rats caused the loss. Now that he had the opportunity, Harvey reasoned that he'd use a stray cat to rid himself of the remaining rats living in his shed—the ones he hadn't been able to trap. That opportunity happened to be me.

So with that idea in mind, still holding me tightly with one hand, he opened the outside door to the shed, tossed me inside, and slammed the door shut. "I'll let you out tomorrow," Harvey shouted as he turned and walked toward the front of the diner. "Get rid of them rats!"

His demand intimidated me, and I felt as though I was one of his kitchen staff and had to follow orders if I wanted to remain employed.

Being thrown into the shed, I landed upright on top of a large sack of potatoes. There was one overhead lightbulb in the center of the room dimly lighting the interior, giving it a dingy, eerie appearance as it swung slightly from side to side from the closing force of the outside door. The light was normally left on because there was no on-off switch near the doorway. It was switched on and off by a pull-chain hanging down from the light fixture.

I slowly looked around the shed in the shallow light in order to get my bearings. The first thing I noticed were the wooden storage shelves that went from floor to ceiling on all four walls. Bags of flour, sugar, and coffee were stacked on the bottom shelves. Pots, fry pans, kettles, and cooking utensils hung from steel hooks. There were also cakes, breads, rolls, pasta, and other food products in covered transparent canisters, as well as ground black pepper and salt in large plastic containers and ketchup in bottles and cans. Lying on the upper shelves were cans of corn, peas, and beans exhibiting their well-imaged labels, just to mention a few of the other items stored. There were even a few scraps of raw stew meat that Harvey had forgotten about and left on a small chopping block. I figured that Harvey had intended to throw out the leftover scraps, but in his haste to grab me, he had forgotten about them, just like he had forgotten to close the lid on the dumpster.

As I scoured my surroundings, I caught the movement of something in the shadows. I focused my attention toward the corner of the shed and that's when I saw it—a very large rat!

Everything had happened so quickly. One moment, I had been outside looking for food. In another moment, I was in a place where there was plenty of food, but it was not where I wanted to be. It was like having a job I did not ask for nor want, and then having to contend with one big rat as part of that unwanted job. This is the same situation we can all face at times—in so many ways!

The large rat approached, and I recognized him from his size and those familiar ruby-colored eyes. It was Amos. "Oh, not again," I mumbled out loud to myself, remembering my previous unpleasant experience with that same rat.

Amos slowly and methodically made his way toward me, but not in the menacing way that I remembered from our first encounter.

"Hey, I've seen you before," he stated as he slowly came face to face with me.

Not knowing what his next move was going to be, I replied as simply as I could. "Yup, we met in the dumpster...a while back." After a brief pause from such an eloquent and witty remark, I added, "I didn't get any supper on that first day I met you, and you made the point I should leave the dumpster. At least I didn't fall on top of you this time." I thought my additional comment was being quite diplomatic about the whole thing and hoped he would perhaps appreciate the levity about not crushing him into some garbage once again.

"Well, there wasn't enough food for everyone that day, and we were there first," Amos replied. "Ya know how it is. This ain't a good situation for either one of us. If we're gonna be confined together, we should try to get along. We have the same goal in mind—food. Harvey doesn't like us because we eat his food, and we also mess up his kitchen whenever we get the chance—on purpose, I might add."

"Why do you mess up his kitchen?"

"Well, mostly because he sets out traps to catch or kill us. We consider it a form of payback. We lost a few of our relatives that way. Not a good way to go, if you know what I mean. It makes for a real bad day for all of us, especially for the one who gets caught."

"I remember a friend of mine talking about mice and rat traps while we were exploring and chasing mice one day," I replied, thinking about one of my excursions with Chester. "It doesn't sound like the use of a trap is a nice thing to do, nor a pleasant way to go." I winced at the thought of being hurt by a trap and sympathized with Amos about the loss of his relatives.

Upon overhearing the conversation, two other rats approached. I recognized them to be the same ones I had seen previously with Amos. To my surprise, Amos introduced them to me. He hadn't done that before. Then he introduced himself once again, unsure if I remembered his name. "My name is Amos, and this is my brother Ollie and my sister Olive." Then they individually proceeded to tell me how their mother had named each of them. They thought it was an amusing story to tell.

I thought Amos seemed like a strange name for a rat. His mother had gotten the idea for his name from a discarded cookie wrapper, one of those advertised famous cookies— you know, one of the great brand names. His brother, Ollie, got his name from an old torn discarded lollipop wrapper with the first letter "L" missing. His mother saw the word "ollipop," and by simply leaving off the letters "pop," decided to call him Ollie. His sister, Olive—well, you can figure that out fairly quickly. It came from the torn label of a discarded, empty olive oil bottle.

Their names, however, weren't based upon anything quite as famous as their brother Amos' name. After all, he was the oldest and the largest of the three. So, in my mind, he was the most prominent rat among them. I politely listened to their stories and then reintroduced myself and told them how I had lost my home and that I had been abandoned. We had quite a chatting session.

After several hours passed, we could hear Harvey in the kitchen, preparing to cook the evening's meals for customers. The back wall of the shed shared the same wall as half of the kitchen and half of the diner's eating area. It covered the entire width of the diner. The rats had chewed several small peepholes in the wall that separated the shed from the diner. They could sit on a shelving unit on one side and look into the diner while people were eating. They could also sit on the other side and watch Harvey cooking in the kitchen. It was like watching a television program for an evening of comic entertainment.

Harvey would always fuss about something not going right in the kitchen, and there was always a customer or two in the dining room who would provide a good show as well. There were obstinate children who refused to eat their suppers and spit out their food, spilled their drinks onto the table, and picked up spaghetti with their fingers and dropped pieces onto the floor. There were also those whiny customers who complained about food being overcooked or undercooked, about the bill being too high, or about the service being slow and having to wait too long for their meals, whether or not it was true. Whether it was Harvey's mishaps or his customers' rebukes, it always made an interesting evening of entertainment for the three rats.

After listening to several of the episodes about the restaurant, I told Amos that his stories were humorous. I developed a rapport with him as I said, "Well, Amos, whether Harvey likes it or not, I have no intention of trying to chase you and your relatives out of here." I guess that's all I really needed to say in order to gain his confidence and friendship.

"I'm glad to hear that," he replied. "I don't see why we can't get along. Like I said before, we all have the same goals in mind. We all want to eat and have a place to live. It's too bad you weren't smaller so you could use our tunnel. Then you could come and go as you please. After Harvey had the drain pipe installed to prevent another flooding incident, he tried to plug it up when he found out we were using it to gain access to this storage shed. But right after that, he had another pipe burst in the diner, and it flooded the bottom of this shed once again because the water couldn't escape. So for a second time, Harvey had a lot of ruined food. He never tried to plug the drain again."

As we talked, Amos' brother, Ollie, developed a mischievous expression on his face. He turned toward Amos and said, "Let's show Patches how we can liven up the entertainment for tonight." Ollie was all excited with the thought of making Harvey's life just a bit more intolerable, at least for the night. Ollie thought playing a joke on Harvey's cooking abilities would be a reasonable return for the anguish that Harvey always caused them by throwing things at them and trying to get rid of them by any means.

"Okay, sounds like fun—let's do something," Amos replied. "Since this is Patches' first night of live entertainment, we should put on a good show."

"We just love to torment Harvey," Olive chimed in.

I continued to sit on the sack of potatoes and watched my new friends with curiosity. The first thing Ollie did was hide some of the kitchen utensils, including ladles and spatulas, behind some of the pots and pans. Then he nudged several of Harvey's larger frying pans toward the back part of the shelves so he'd have to get on a stool to reach them.

"I have a great idea," said Amos with a wide grin and a glint in his eyes. "Where's that lettuce, tomato, and cucumber salad bowl that Harvey mixed up earlier and left out here?"

"It's over on the third shelf up," replied Ollie. "Why, what do you want with that?"

"You'll see," said Amos anxiously. He then quickly ran up the side of the wooden shelf and sat on the edge of the large mixing bowl full of salad, facing away from the center of the bowl. Olive followed behind him to see what he was doing.

"You're—In the salad!" Olive exclaimed, astonished at what she was seeing her brother doing and not completing what she intended to say before Amos interrupted her. He knew Olive would be disgusted by what she saw him doing.

"Yup!" Amos replied, proud of his accomplishment and still straining during his somewhat shameful act. "To make it sound nice, you could call it excrement. That's a much nicer term than what I think you were going to use!"

Olive nodded a yes to Amos' comment.

"The customers will think Harvey put raisins in their salad. Wait till they bite down on these morsels of intense flavor! How yummy!" Amos exclaimed.

Olive grimaced at the thought of anyone eating the salad. "That smell is just plain rank," she said. "What in the world did you eat yesterday?"

"I only ate what Harvey cooked and threw out as leftovers. He's basically getting back what he kinda gave us, only in a different form—same kind of crap, though." Amos snickered at his innuendo.

Olive paused for a moment, thinking about what Amos said. "Oh, I get it. I know what you mean."

At the thought of what he was doing and the eventual repercussions his actions would cause, Amos added, "I've had a lot of indigestion and gas all day because of his food. It's time to get even."

"I hope the smell goes away before anyone realizes those aren't raisins," Olive replied.

"Yeah, remember when we did something similar all over Harvey's kitchen one afternoon?" exclaimed Ollie. "A health inspector visited the diner right after we finished and noticed our rat droppings during the inspection. It couldn't have been a better time for an unannounced visit. He made Harvey sanitize the entire diner and threatened to close his business if he didn't comply with a proper clean up. It took Harvey over two days to sanitize everything and clean up the little 'raisin' mess we made. We left them on plates, in coffee cups, in his dry pasta bowls—just about everywhere we could think of. The three of us did a better job than any number of rabbits could have done. But we never thought to do it in his salads. This will be a real surprise. It actually took Harvey even more time to scrape up the grease in his dirty kitchen than it did for him to clean up the dirty mess we made before the inspector was satisfied. So we actually did a real public service act for the people who eat here. At least that prank resulted in a more sanitary kitchen."

"Quick," Amos said to Olive. "Jump into the bowl and mix this all up so Harvey doesn't see these 'raisins' on top." Olive didn't hesitate. She jumped into the large container, mixed up all the ingredients in the salad with all four feet going at once, and then quickly jumped out of the bowl.

"Is that mixed enough?" she asked.

"Looks good to me. He'll never notice. Ollie, get a little of that ketchup out and smear it on Patches' whiskers."

"What on earth for?"

"You'll see," said Amos, wearing a knowing smirk on his face.

I just sat there, not knowing why Ollie was dribbling ketchup leaking from a leftover container onto my whiskers.

Figuring there must be a good reason for it, I wasn't going to second-guess him.

Just as Ollie finished with the ketchup, we could hear Harvey approach the door from the kitchen to the shed. Just in time, I thought, as one by one, all three rats scampered into the top of the drainpipe so they couldn't be seen. I remained sitting on the potato sack, not happy about the taste of the ketchup dripping from my whiskers and into a corner of my mouth. I sat there wondering what was going to happen next.

Chapter 9

The Prank

Harvey came into the storage shed from the diner's kitchen and immediately went over to one of the shelves where he kept a few of his large frying pans. Ollie had guessed correctly. He had nudged the frying pans so far to the back of the shelf that Harvey couldn't reach them. Harvey glanced in my direction and muttered under his breath as if he were talking to me, "Why do I always put these pans up so far to the back of the shelves that I can't reach them? I don't get it. I do it all the time. Every time I come out to get one of these pans, I have to get the stepladder out. I don't ever remember using the ladder to put them there in the first place, though."

He retrieved the ladder from the corner of the shed, set it against the shelving unit, and climbing two steps up, reached for one of the frying pans. With his other hand, he grabbed the salad that was sitting on a lower shelf, containing the new ingredient of "raisins."

Just as Harvey was returning the ladder, he looked at me still sitting on the sack of potatoes, noticed my red whiskers, and then quickly looked around the shed. There were no signs of any rats. "Hey, big boy. Looks like you got at least one of them rats for me already—good job. And you ate one of 'em too, huh? You stay in here tonight and look for more of them. I'll get you something better to eat later, and I'll let you out of here tomorrow."

Harvey was happy with the thought that the rat population in his shed looked like it had been reduced by at least one rat. He left the shed with the salad bowl and the frying pan. As he returned to the kitchen, I could hear the bell over the entrance to the front door of the diner jingle as customers started to arrive for their evening meal.

Upon hearing Harvey slam the door from the shed to the kitchen, Amos and his siblings peeked up over the top of the drainpipe to make sure it was safe to come out.

"Good job, big boy," Amos repeated, mocking Harvey's comment and laughing at me with the ketchup still dripping from my whiskers.

"Can I get rid of this awful tasting ketchup?" I asked.

"Sure thing. I'll wipe that stuff off for you," said Olive as she yanked a napkin off one of the shelves and managed to wipe off the excess ketchup dripping from my whiskers.

"Is everyone ready for some entertainment?" Ollie asked.

"This should be interesting to watch," said Olive.

The three rats climbed up to the fifth shelf on the wall facing the diner.

"Come on up and take a peek at this," Amos shouted to me with noticeable anticipation in his voice. With little effort, I jumped from the potato sack up onto a shelf with my newly acquired friends and took my first peek through one of the small holes that were chewed through the thin sheet rock wall. Looking through the tiny peepholes, you could see the entire dining room area. Unlike many traditional diners, the service counter was smaller than most others and was separated from the restaurant's food preparation area. Most of the kitchen couldn't be seen by the customers and was completely separated from the eating area. There were floor-mounted stools for the customers sitting along the service counter and two rows of booths that ran the entire length of the diner.

Old man Clement was the first patron to arrive at a booth nearest the back wall separating the storage shed from the diner. He was a retired welder, in his late seventies. His thick, bushy gray eyebrows and short-cropped beard enhanced the features of his thin, weatherworn face and gave him a very distinctive appearance. His language, in contrast, was coarse, crude, and sometimes rude, perhaps to the point where most people didn't like eating with him or even being near him for that matter. He didn't have many friends and ate alone most of the time. Very few people could tolerate his rough, caustic demeanor. He ate alone at the diner every Friday night with few exceptions. The rats liked to watch Clement because they never knew what he would do or say next to either the waiter or anyone that happened to be sitting at a nearby table.

"Watch what happens with this guy," Amos remarked. I huddled next to my new friends in order to share the few available peepholes. With our eyes pressed closely to the wall, we focused our attention on the dining room.

The waiter approached Clement. "What'll you have tonight, Mr. Clement?"

"I'm gonna have my usual—the spaghetti with meatballs and a salad with Italian dressing."

The waiter hurriedly wrote down the order and was relieved there was no further discussion. He had waited on Clement many times before and never knew what to expect from the old "geezer"—the term the waiter used to describe Clement. Sometimes, Clement would go through each menu item, asking questions and complaining about the prices. Then he would order his usual. Tonight, he said nothing more to the waiter.

"Okay, I'll be right back with your order, Mr. Clement. Do you want the salad first, or would you like it with your spaghetti?"

"Just bring me everything at once," replied Clement.

The audience was getting restless, knowing what was about to happen. Old man Clement had ordered a salad with his meal. The rats couldn't have picked a better victim. The wait seemed like an eternity, but in about ten minutes, the waiter returned with Clement's entire meal.

"Here we go," said Ollie excitedly. It was like going to a movie that was about to begin, waiting for the lights to dim in anticipation of the feature film. We positioned ourselves in front of the peepholes in order to get the best possible view of Clement.

"Here's your order," said the waiter as he placed Clement's plate of spaghetti and a small bowl of salad in front of him. "Can I get you anything else to drink besides the water?"

"Nope," replied Clement. "This will do."

Clement started with the spaghetti, winding several thick strands of pasta around his fork and then thoughtfully adding a piece of meatball. He took a sip of water and then stuck his fork into the salad.

We actually shook with excitement, knowing that the climax to our movie could happen at any moment and that something bad was about to happen. Our anxiety heightened as Clement lifted the fork from the salad bowl. It had captured a large amount of lettuce, cucumber, tomato, and buried within the lettuce, you could see several "raisins". Clement put the entire fork, full of the newly seasoned salad, into his mouth and chewed. He didn't chew for long, though. As soon as he bit into the "raisins," he spit out the entire mouthful. It was as if a geyser had suddenly erupted all over the table and into his plate of spaghetti. The pieces went everywhere, even onto the floor.

"That's awful!" Clement exclaimed loudly without even thinking or caring that everyone in the diner could hear him.

The waiter who had taken his order was serving a customer at another table at the time. Startled by the loud outburst, he quickly excused himself and rushed over to find out what the problem was. "What's wrong?" he asked Clement.

"The raisins in this salad are rancid. They taste like crap and smell like something that came out of an overflowing septic tank!" There was no mincing of words with Clement. It was just the way he was—direct and to the point. That's why the rats considered him to be a good victim for their prank.

The anguish on the waiter's face said it all. He had to put up with Clement once again and listen to his ranting. It seemed like there was always some sort of issue every Friday night with the old man. But with restrained effort, the waiter still remembered his manners and what his job entailed, and he apologized to Clement. "I'm so very sorry, Mr. Clement. I'll take your salad back to the kitchen and ask Harvey about it." He noticed pieces of lettuce and tomato dangling from the top of the meatballs and quickly added, "I'll also get you a fresh plate of spaghetti."

Clement, however, had few manners. His response was curt. "Yeah, you do that. Make sure the salad is either fresh this time or forget about the salad entirely. I'm certainly not going to eat that or anything like it again, and I'm certainly not going to pay for it. Those raisins are the worst I've ever eaten—just plain awful. And who puts raisins in a salad any-way? When did Harvey start putting raisins in his salads?"

The waiter shook his head from side to side, indicating he didn't have an answer to Clement's question. He took the sal-ad bowl and the plate that resembled a spaghetti dinner that had been bombarded by a vegetable garden and quickly en-tered the kitchen through the double swinging doors. Amos, Ollie, Olive, and I quickly moved from our perch overlooking the eating area of the diner onto another shelf overlooking the kitchen area so we could watch Harvey's reaction.

There were peepholes in that section of the wall as well. It was kind of like watching a basketball game, looking from one side of the court to another in order to catch all the action.

"Harvey, old man Clement says the raisins in the salad you made are rancid!" exclaimed the waiter as he thrust the salad bowl in front of Harvey.

"I didn't put any raisins in the salad," replied Harvey. "What's that crazy old coot talking about this time? We go through some sort of issue with him every week. He's never happy with anything. Give me that bowl. Let's see it."

Harvey grabbed the bowl from the waiter, carefully ob-serving the brownish morsels scattered throughout the let-tuce and held in place by the Italian salad dressing. "What are these?" he questioned.

The poor waiter was speechless.

Harvey picked up a piece of lettuce containing the uni-dentified morsels with his fingers and chewed it. The expres-sion on his face was priceless. "That's just got to be rat poop!" he exclaimed.

The waiter winced at the thought of the tainted food.

Ollie laughed so hard he almost fell off the shelf.

"Those darn rats!" Harvey declared, as his face flushed with anger. "They ruined all that salad that I made earlier. I hope that cat gets all of them for this!"

Luckily, Clement didn't hear Harvey's loud exclamation regarding rat poop. Otherwise, he would have been eating free meals for a while after threatening to report the incident to the state health inspector. Harvey wouldn't want to go through that inspection process again—once before was enough.

Harvey quickly sent the waiter back to Clement's table with a fresh salad, a fresh plate of pasta, an apology, and a message from Harvey that Clement would be given the meal for free for his inconvenience. Nothing was mentioned about the 'raisins'.

After the initial excitement had subsided, I could only think of one thing to say to my new entertainment committee. "That was a great show." We all laughed so hard it looked as if we were crying. In that single moment, I managed to forget about the sadness that haunted me from day to day.

We spent the rest of the evening going from one viewing area to another, watching people eating and listening to Harvey complaining about things going wrong in the kitchen. Even Clement left the restaurant that night with a smile on his face, just happy he had gotten a free dinner.

After the diner closed, we talked for several hours about all the things we saw happen that night. Amos and his siblings eventually decided to get some sleep and hid behind some large sacks of flour and sugar so that Harvey wouldn't see them. I fell asleep on one of the shelves next to the diner's wall. It was much warmer there than sleeping outside in my cardboard box shelter in back of the clothing store. Before retiring for the night, Harvey kept his promise and left some table scraps on the shelf next to me. I was surprised he was that thoughtful. Sometimes, I guess, there's a little good in everyone.

It was late when Harvey finally locked up for the night. He didn't have far to go in order to get home, however, because he lived alone in a small apartment next door to the diner. He kept his promise the following morning and released me from the storage shed, erroneously thinking that I had eliminated at least a few rats. For several days afterwards, Amos, Ollie, Olive, and I laughed at the very thought of that night's events. I'll never forget it. After that night, it shouldn't be any surprise to you that I was the only stray cat in the neighborhood who was allowed to eat with the rats without any concerns, even in the dumpster.

As time progressed, I gradually started to fit in with the daily routines of my new environment and became very familiar with my part of the neighborhood. I seldom ever wandered further than a ten-block radius. That part of the town, where I wandered from day to day, was my whole world. I often went from door to door searching for something to eat or searching for alternative shelters from the weather. But even though I was considered "cute" by some people's viewpoint, no one took me into their homes as a permanent resident. It didn't matter what I looked like. The economy was still slow, apparently not improving, and unemployment continued to rise. The people in the neighborhood found it difficult enough to feed themselves, let alone try to take care of any pets. Most people just couldn't afford to feed an extra mouth, and some people just didn't care.

I never returned to the old two-story rundown house where I was born. I thought about it a lot, but Henry's words had taken their toll. I found it difficult to deal with the fact that I wasn't wanted. Memories of my siblings started to fade, and the thought of forgetting them worried me. I didn't know where they were. The one thing I clearly did remember, though, was the image of my mother, and our reflection together in the broken pieces of that old hand-mirror. I often thought about her warmth and constant attention. I missed the security I once had, and most of all, I missed the unconditional love she shared with me. I had good days and bad days, just like everyone else does on occasion. It's all part of life.

The month of October had more good days than bad days, however, and proved to be beneficial in acquiring new friends. Not only had I become an unlikely companion to three rats, but I also found a new friend during my daily travels that month, as well as an unconventional meeting with a neighborhood bully.

Chapter 10

A New Friend

A cat named Buster lived in the hallways and basement of one of the old brick tenement buildings that lined one side of the street that I often traveled. He lived almost directly across the street from Carlo—you know, the mean dog I mentioned earlier. Buster was deemed to be the tenement building's cat, because most of the tenants knew him. Even though he lived with no one family in particular, many of the tenants put food out for him in the hallways by their apartments. They all liked Buster. He was the residents' cat.

Buster was twice my size, very muscular for a cat, and weighed a good twenty-five pounds or so. Most animals avoided Buster whenever they could, mostly because they feared his size and reputation of being a fighter. Even the dogs in the neighborhood wouldn't mess with him. He kept his claws sharp and kept in shape by chasing gray squirrels up and down the few trees that lined the sidewalks. He was never interested in catching any of them, just chasing them. If any animals in the neighborhood picked a fight with Buster, they usually ended up looking like a prize-fighter who had just lost ten rounds of their worst fight. His name was a good fit for his character. He never started a fight, but he could "bust" up just about any fight there was. He was the proverbial lean, mean, fighting machine—but only when it was necessary.

Buster didn't like any cats, that is, not until he met me. For some reason, though, he liked me almost from the start, and we became good friends. Perhaps he felt bad for me once he learned how I had come to wander the streets by myself, not unlike his own story in many ways. Perhaps he saw a bit of compassion in me that he himself had, but kept hidden underneath his rugged exterior. Perhaps, it was just the unusual way we met when he accidentally bumped into me, causing the chance meeting to be entirely his fault.

It happened on one particular day when I was just passing the staircase in front of the tenement building where Buster lived. A fight broke out on the front stoop between Buster and a short-haired tiger cat named Murray. Murray wasn't very smart by any means, especially when he made the conscious decision to pick a fight with Buster. Murray lived two buildings down from Buster, and I think the quarrel was based upon a territorial issue. I don't know what else it could have been. The problem, however, was that it was Buster's territory that Murray had invaded, not the other way around. Buster lived there, Murray didn't. The issue was as simple as that.

Murray slunk up on Buster and tackled him while he was asleep. A quarrel ensued, and they tumbled down the old granite stairs, kicking furiously at each other and body-slamming into me just as I was passing by the front steps. The combined weight of both cats, locked together with front and back feet kicking each other, knocked me off the curbing into the street.

The combined collision resulted in a momentary separation of the fighting duo. At that point, I think Murray figured he was going to lose the battle that he shouldn't have started in the first place. So Murray got to his feet, righted himself, and quickly ran off down the street back to where he lived. The collision was a good thing for Murray, however, because it gave him the opportunity to flee without further retaliation from Buster, and at the same time allowed him to save what little self-esteem he had left.

Buster watched Murray as he escaped down the sidewalk and fleeted homeward. He then turned around to face me and just stood there on the sidewalk waiting to see what I was going to do next. I guess his first thought was that I was going to challenge him for territory or for some sort of reprisal. He was anticipating another fight and was ready for it.

Getting back up onto the sidewalk and shaking my head

slightly from side to side, I regained my balance and my composure. I approached Buster, who was ready to continue defending his home turf, and asked, "What was that all about?"

My question was so sudden and impromptu that Buster didn't know how to respond. He just assumed nothing would be said and some sort of squabble would ensue without any further discussion. Apparently, no one had ever confronted Buster with a question before, under any circumstances—no one, ever. Upon asking the question, I noticed the muscles in his body seem to relax, and he stood there looking at me trying to think of what he was going to say next. There was a long pause as Buster turned to watch Murray running away, and then he turned to look at me once again.

I'll never forget his first words to me.

"Nothing worse than a stupid cat," he muttered.

"What do you mean?" I asked.

"That idiot knows this is my home turf, yet he always starts a fight. He's just a bully that doesn't know any better. I just get so tired of trying to teach him over and over again that this is my place. He's soooo stupid! I really don't like stupid cats." Buster thought for a moment and then changed the subject. "Are you a stray?" he asked, as if he were trying to decide whether I was friend or foe. "I've seen you wandering around these tenement buildings before, but I never thought much about it until now."

"Yeah, I've been out on the streets for a little while now. I guess we've just never crossed each other's paths or never have taken the opportunity to speak to each other until now," I replied, perhaps gaining a little sympathy with my answer.

"Well, tumbling into you like we did and involving you in a fight that wasn't yours is not the best of conditions for having to cross each other's paths. Why don't you tell me a bit about yourself and why I've only seen you around here just recently? There's a nice, warm sunny spot near the top of the stairs. Let's talk."

I was still a little dazed from the impact of two fighting cats having their combined weight force me off the sidewalk. But it was the surprise of the sudden impact that had more of an effect than anything else did, and I thought it might be a good idea to sit and talk for a bit. As I climbed the stairs with Buster, I could feel the sunshine as it reflected off the brick facade of the tenement building and onto the stoop at the top of the stairs, adding warmth to the front entrance. Sitting on nice, warm granite sounded like a good idea to me.

"You two were really going at it," I said as we reached the top of the stairs.

"Yeah, sorry we tumbled into you like we did. Every once in a while, that bully gets the insane idea to challenge me. I have several advantages, though, but he never seems to understand that. I weigh more than he does, I'm stronger than he is, and I also have a lot more knowledge in how to defend myself than he does. That's evident 'cause he always loses the fights he starts with me."

Our conversation continued into the afternoon as we sat on the building's small granite landing that led to the front entrance and enjoyed the sun. We spent several hours talking about our lives and how we came to be where we were. While we talked, I noticed the old man I had seen on previous occasions. He was still wearing the same dirty T-shirt, tattered coat, and dilapidated shoes. I had seen him earlier in the day rummaging through the same garbage cans once again, and decided to ask Buster if the old man was homeless. I was curious.

"His name is Tate. That's basically all I know about him," replied Buster. "I think he's a World War II veteran, and he's homeless just like us. Every once in a while I see him collecting cardboard in order to make a shelter to keep out of the weather. He sleeps in various locations, very seldom ever the same place. He doesn't have a permanent home. I guess you might call him a vagabond."

Our similarities as abandoned cats provided a unique bond in our relationship, and it only took a few weeks before we ultimately became good friends. Buster had lived on the streets for as long as he could remember, and the best he could recollect was that he was at least nine years old.

Our chance meeting that day, similar to my first encounter with Chester, was a helpful one for me. In the weeks to follow, Buster taught me how to climb trees, sharpen my claws on tree trunks, and how to wrestle other cats in case I had to protect myself. He even taught me a very useful hammerlock hold that worked well in dissuading other cats from being aggressive. That sort of wrestling maneuver would put another cat in a position so that it was difficult and almost impossible to carry on a fight.

Buster's lessons didn't stop with wrestling, though. He also taught me to be gentle and kind to small or helpless animals. Buster had been bullied as a kitten by stray cats who lived in the vicinity of the tenement building. As he became larger and stronger, he remembered those experiences and always looked out for the wellbeing of smaller animals by protecting them from those same bullies.

Buster's kindness was demonstrated one day when a kitten who lived in one of the apartments had managed to get outside without anyone knowing about it and had climbed up a maple tree in front of the tenement building. Once he got up onto a high, overhanging branch, however, he couldn't figure out how to get down. Without hesitation and before the kitten could fall from his precarious perch, Buster climbed the tree, grabbed the kitten by the loose skin on the back of his neck, and gently with his teeth carried the kitten down the tree.

Since the front door to the building was usually open, Buster carried the kitten into the building, placed him in front of the apartment door where he lived, and scratched on the door. Once he heard someone coming, he quickly left before being seen. I was there to observe the entire rescue, and only I knew that Buster was a hero that day. Buster, of course, didn't want anyone to know he had a soft spot of compassion surrounding his tough exterior. He didn't want something like that to ruin his reputation.

Saving the kitten by grabbing him by the scruff of the neck taught me an invaluable lesson that day. It was a lesson I eventually used myself.

During one of our bonding sessions, I found out how Buster had become proficient with his fighting and defensive maneuvers. We were sitting on the small stoop of the tenement building, like we did on several sunny afternoons, when three young boys came walking down the sidewalk. As they passed in front of us, they all spoke to Buster, then proceeded to walk around the corner of the building. I recognized them as the three J's.

"I've seen those boys before," I said to Buster. "They're a group of boys who call themselves the three J's. My father and I saw them exercising together in the woods where we lived. How do they know you?"

"One of those boys lives in this building," replied Buster. "He and his mother put food out in the hallway for me from time to time. Because of that, they all know me by name. The short kid on the left is Jessie. He's the one who lives in this building. He's on the wrestling team at his school. The one in the middle is Jason. He takes Karate lessons. And the tall kid on the right is Jake. He goes to a local fitness center, studies Tai Chi, and learns from the other two. They all practice different forms of exercise together as a group. That's probably why they call themselves the three J's."

"What do you mean about Jake learning from the other two?" I asked.

"Follow me. I'll show you," replied Buster as he ambled down the stairs and onto the sidewalk. I followed him, and we proceeded behind the three boys around the side of the building.

There was a wooden bulkhead at the rear of Buster's tenement building that led to the basement. We watched as all three boys struggled to open the bulkhead door and disappeared into the basement. The wooden bulkhead had warped from the cold, wet weather over the years, making it difficult to open. It didn't always shut easily either. Sometimes the door was latched and locked from the outside, so a person couldn't access the basement. In most instances, however, even if the door was locked, you could usually squeeze through a small opening on one side of the bulkhead where a section of the wood was rotten.

The door wasn't locked that afternoon, and once the boys managed to swing open the bulkhead, we followed the three J's down the cement stairs.

The basement was expansive and made up of old stone walls and a concrete floor. It was filled with all sorts of things discarded by previous tenants. There was furniture, including old chairs and sofas, stacks of magazines, and all sorts of storage containers stacked in random places throughout the gray expanse. Scattered throughout the area were newspapers, old bed sheets used as drop cloths for painting, and rags used for cleanup.

If Buster couldn't manage to get into the main part of the building through the front entrance to sleep in one of the hallways, he would often sleep in the basement. It was his sanctuary. He had taken advantage of some of the remnants left behind and had made himself a comfortable sleeping spot from old sheets that he had gathered together on top of one of the storage containers. His prefabricated bed was hidden in a back corner by an ancient, oil-fired furnace that provided steam heat to the six floors of apartments.

Looking around this wondrous cavern of accumulated junk, Buster motioned me toward the back corner of the basement where we jumped up on his makeshift bed and sat there watching the three J's start their Tai Chi forms. The boys had cleared an area and had unrolled an old rug that gave them plenty of space to practice. After several evolutions of Tai Chi, they proceeded to practice some wrestling holds. That's the first time I saw the usefulness of the hammerlock hold. Buster had learned a lot by watching the boys practice and, in turn, he taught me.

After a while, the boys stopped and sat down on an old sofa. They talked about their homework, teachers, and upcoming school events. It was then that I saw each of them remove a small paper cylinder from a package that Jessie pulled from his jacket pocket.

"What are they doing now?" I asked Buster.

"They're smoking cigarettes. To them, it's a social thing to do together. After they light those things on fire, they inhale the smoke and then exhale it back out. It's not really good for them, and I'm sure their parents don't know they're doing it. I'll tell you one thing, though. Their parents aren't gonna like it if they catch them smoking. They could get into a lot of trouble if they find out, especially at their age. Tate, the old homeless man, also smokes. If you're around him some time, listen to that real nasty cough he has. I think it's from smoking too many of the half-finished cigarettes he finds on the streets."

We watched as the three teenage boys finished smoking their cigarettes, crushed them out on the concrete floor to extinguish them, and left the basement. We stayed behind, and I got my first afternoon nap in the warm basement next to the furnace. It was a nice reprieve from the cool October air that consistently whistled through the gaps of my cardboard condo. The basement of that tenement building was a great place to hide, to play, and to cat-nap on cold, rainy afternoons. It's also the place where Buster taught me a lot of wrestling maneuvers. We spent many days practicing together as well as watching the three J's exercise and practice.

Although I hadn't yet experienced living outside in the snow and cold, I knew I would have to face an oncoming winter. That thought worried me. Some nights I'd return to the alley in back of the clothing store and find that my cardboard house had been removed and taken to the dump for recycling. There were other nights when the chill from nightly downpours forced me to find alternative shelters because my entire soggy condo would collapse. Under those conditions, if I couldn't manage to find a way into Harvey's storage shed by the diner, Buster would share his lodgings with me. When the weather was that bad, Buster's basement home gave me another option for shelter.

During the last week of October, I met another new friend. However, instead of meeting by chance, as I had with Buster, we met because of a careless and dangerous mistake.

Chapter 11

Stupid Dog

I was on my way to visit Buster one afternoon when I spotted a black and tan colored Corgi walking down the sidewalk on the opposite side of the street from me. I recognized him. It was Mr. and Mrs. Hoffstedder's Corgi, Bracken. There he was, on the sidewalk in front of Carlo's yard, not a particularly smart place to be. His ears were flapping in the breeze as he trotted along, happily and nonchalantly observing the world around him, and not paying any attention as to where he was going; nothing out of the ordinary for Bracken.

That silly dog, I thought as I started up the stairs of the tenement building to see if Buster was sleeping in the sun on the front stoop. I had seen Bracken out walking on several occasions, so it wasn't unusual for him to be out and about. Mr. Hoffstedder's wife Dora often let Bracken out of the house without a leash so he could go to the bathroom by himself. As a result of his newfound freedom, he sometimes took the opportunity to wander the streets for a few hours before returning home. I think he just felt good to get out and wander around.

I was only halfway up the stairs of the tenement building when I heard Carlo's familiar growl and instinctively knew something was amiss. I looked up the staircase, and Buster was nowhere to be seen. Then I turned around to see what the commotion was all about. What I witnessed was more than just disturbing—the sight sent chills throughout my senses. Looking across the street, I saw that the small dog had managed to get himself into an unpredictable dilemma. Regardless of whether or not Carlo was leashed so he couldn't reach the mailbox in the front yard, the mailman always dashed in and out of Carlo's yard as if his life depended upon it. If Carlo was in a bad mood and he wasn't on a short leash, the mailman figured that he could be in some jeopardy. On this particular day, in his haste, the mailman didn't take the time to latch the front gate properly, and it had swung back open. Bracken didn't notice that Carlo was in the yard and had decided to investigate the newly opened area. As usual, he wasn't paying any attention to where he was going and approached Carlo head-on. He was looking everywhere but straight ahead. After walking nonchalantly through the front gate and down the walkway beyond the mailbox, Bracken heard a deep growl—a growl that not only caught his attention, but caught mine as well. Bracken turned his head toward the sound and was suddenly staring directly at Carlo's knobby knees.

Being a Corgi means you're short, low to the ground, and have vertically challenged vision. So, in Bracken's world, all you normally would see are ankles and knees when approaching larger dogs. It was probably a good thing that Bracken didn't see the gleaming white fangs that went along with Carlo's snarl. The growl itself was intimidating enough, but those teeth—they were just plain scary.

Carlo was many times the size of Bracken and assumed Bracken's obtrusive approach was a direct challenge to his territory. No one would be dumb enough or in their right state of mind to enter Carlo's yard without some sort of invitation. Only a carefree dog like Bracken would do something stupid like that. He was smart enough to realize, however, that he was in trouble and froze in his tracks upon hearing the foreboding growl, afraid to move.

"Oh no!" I shouted, hoping that Buster might hear me. I wondered if he was nearby so he might be able to think of a way to help. Something had to be done and done quickly before Carlo attacked poor Bracken. I knew Carlo would seriously harm the little dog. He'd make mincemeat out of him.

I was becoming a fairly large cat, but even I couldn't protect Bracken from a dog the size of Carlo. Two cats might have a chance, especially with someone like Buster, but he was nowhere to be seen. I alone was certainly no match for such a large adversary. I quickly tried to think of alternative solutions for the situation, and noticed that Carlo was leashed to a post and could only travel so far. But he could still reach poor Bracken, who was standing directly in front of him.

Luckily, I had learned a lot from being on my own, and one of those things was to carefully observe what happened around me on a daily basis. In my wanderings, I had witnessed that some dogs didn't like loud noises. I had seen dogs run from lightning storms and from the sound of thunder. Those types of storms never bothered me—neither the deep rumbles of thunder nor the magnificent light displays from lightning. Even some of the larger dogs turned into wimps during thunderstorms. I always thought it odd that such large animals could be so afraid of such everyday occurrences. I had also seen dogs scamper from the approach of my buddy, Buster. That fear actually made more sense because Buster could be a formidable foe. Of course, he wasn't anywhere in sight, so he was no help. I realized it was time to take responsibility and act quickly.

I had what I thought was a brilliant idea. I noticed a large piece of corrugated sheet metal leaning against the corner of the chain-link fence within Carlo's yard. It was a long piece of metal that extended several feet past the height of the fence. It stood almost vertically and leaned directly against the inside corner. A metal garbage can overflowing with aluminum cans sat directly in front of the long piece of sheet metal.

I heard another deep-pitched growl and looked back toward the two dogs. They were still facing each other. Neither one had moved. There was no time to waste. I knew I had to do something and do it quickly. I ran down the stairs from the tenement building, across the street, and climbed up the chain-link fence to the top. It was the fastest trip from one place to another that I had ever made.

Perched precariously on the top rail of the fence, I pushed the vertical piece of sheet metal with my front feet with all the strength I could muster so that it fell over onto the garbage can. The sheet metal buckled as it wavered at first and then crashed into the garbage can, which in turn toppled over, spilling hundreds of aluminum cans. The sound was horrific. It was as if a sudden lightning storm had struck with all its might, releasing all of its energy in a deafening clap of thunder.

Carlo instinctively spun around and ran for cover. He thought lightning had struck his doghouse. I think everyone could hear his yelp three streets away. He had forgotten about everything else. Bracken was lucky. Carlo happened to be one of those dogs afraid of thunder.

"What was that?" I heard him exclaim as he continued to bark, hoping that someone might come to his rescue.

Bracken was a happy-go-lucky sort of dog, but he wasn't completely stupid in not taking advantage of a forgiving situation. He took that instant moment of diversion to make his escape. He did an about-face, ran for the gate farther than Carlo's leash allowed, and crossed the street onto the opposite sidewalk in front of Buster's tenement building. I was amazed at just how fast those short legs could go.

I jumped down from the fence and ran back across the street to find Bracken out of breath. Actually, we both were. We sat on the curb with a sigh of relief. Facing Carlo's yard, I could just barely see him hiding behind his doghouse, probably wondering when the next clap of thunder would come.

Buster appeared from the back of his building just in time to find both of us contemplating the success of my rescue mission.

"Now you show up," I said to Buster as I noticed his approach. "I could have used your help a few minutes ago."

"I heard the raucous," Buster responded, "but I guess I was too late for the show. I was around the back of the building, trying to get into the basement, when I heard the loud crash out here. There are some trash cans blocking the entrance to the bulkhead, otherwise I wouldn't be out here now. I was just in time to see what happened. Looks like you two managed to survive Carlo. Congratulations."

"Luckily, Carlo's afraid of thunderstorms, even if they are cat created," I replied. "Nothing worse than a stupid dog."

"Now that sounds like something I'd say." Buster grinned, remembering his earlier comments about Murray. "He's just like Murray. He's a bully that doesn't know any better. Look at him trying to hide behind his doghouse over there. You're right—stupid dog! Good thing, though, huh?"

At that moment, I turned to Bracken, who was noticeably

still frightened and panting heavily from the encounter. I gave him two pieces of advice that I myself had learned within only a few short weeks. "I need to tell you something that you should always keep in mind. Size might matter sometimes, but there are times when size and strength can be overtaken by using your wit. This was a good example of that." And then with a slight smile, I added, "One more thing, it's also a good idea to pay attention to where you're going." There wasn't much more Bracken could do or say as he carefully considered the consequences of his actions. He reluctantly agreed with me.

Those words must have had some effect because it was the last time Bracken walked in front of Carlo's house without watching where he was going. It was difficult to forget such an experience. He was warned not to do it again, and as far as I know, he never did. Sometimes, you can reason with others, and sometimes you can't. There are those times when no matter how much you reason, the outcome will remain the same. But at least you should try.

Bracken and I became friends after that experience. You might think it's a strange combination, a cat and a dog getting along together and becoming friends. But it does happen, sometimes. Just like people—you may come from different backgrounds and have different opinions about things, but that doesn't mean you can't be friends or share some of the same principles.

The months of November and December were a new experience for me. I had never before lived outside in the winter. The constant cold of sunless days and freezing temperatures found me huddled within my cardboard lodgings at night. I tried to keep myself busy having daily romps with Chester, Buster, Bracken, and the rats at the diner. Every once in a while I'd sit with Amos and his siblings watching Harvey cooking in the kitchen or watching the customers in the diner eating their meals and complaining about the food, especially Mr. Clement.

The rats continued to pull pranks on Harvey, and it was always entertaining. I never grew tired of their antics. But as the weather grew colder, I realized I didn't have a semi-permanent home like everyone else seemed to have. I was always the visitor. Sometimes, whenever I could manage to get into the storage shed at the diner on my own or when Harvey thought it was time I could help rid his storage shed of rats, I would stay with Amos, Ollie, and Olive.

Sometimes I would sleep in the basement of the tenement building with Buster if the bulkhead door was left ajar or the side of the bulkhead wasn't blocked.

There were other times, however, when the bulkhead to the basement of the tenement building would be shut, locked tight, and inaccessible, and I had to return to my makeshift cardboard box condominium in the back alley behind the retail clothing store.

Most mornings, though, the bulkhead door was opened at some point in order to store household trash or to stack the previous day's newspapers from the apartments. I would often find Buster asleep on his old sheets and we'd spend part of the day together. At other times, I'd meet Bracken and participate in one of his wandering neighborhood adventures. But I had no place I could call home. I was a vagabond like old man Tate, moving from one place to another, with no permanent home, unlike my friends in that respect.

The holidays of Thanksgiving and Christmas were hard to accept with no family to share them with. But there was plentiful food left over in the dumpster at the diner during those days. I noticed, however, that daylight ended earlier and darkness came much too quickly during the latter part of December, making the cold nights seem to last so much longer. Psychologically, it probably didn't help my frame of mind before returning to my cardboard shelter for the night by checking the large round dial on an outdoor thermometer that hung from the wall next to the front door of the diner. As the dial drifted more toward the lower numbers, I knew my nights would be colder.

Two days after the Christmas holiday, I got my first taste of freezing winter temperatures as the cold air reached zero degrees. Freezing conditions made me realize that the harshness of a New England winter could be dangerous for survival. It snowed, light at first with little moisture, then it turned to freezing rain, and then back to wet, heavy snow.

It was late evening, and I had not been successful in finding a warm, dry place to sleep. The lowly lit street lamps reflected the fog caused by the moisture from drifting snow.

I shivered from the cold slush enveloping my every step, penetrating the pads on my paws and chilling my inner warmth until there simply wasn't any. I could see my breath when I exhaled as my lungs took in cold air and exhausted the precious warmer air into the night. The chill factor from an unrelenting wind was minus twenty degrees, and my small lungs stung from the cold air with every breath I took.

I managed to scrounge up some food from the dumpster, and on my way back from the diner to my wet cardboard box shelter, I stopped at Chester's house. I liked to stop there and watch the birds eating sunflower seeds from the hanging bird feeders under the eaves of the house. Their dances from one feeder to another always helped to take my mind off the harsh realities I faced. I never tried to catch them, though. The birds were trying to survive just like I was, and I enjoyed watching them as they hopped from one bird feeder to another. They reminded me of the day when I found myself staring up at the branches of the big oak tree by the front door of the house where I used to live, watching their unending trips from one branch to another. It made me wonder what it would be like to have a family like Chester had.

Every once in a while I would see Lilly sitting on the inside sill of the large bay window that looked out onto their front lawn as she watched the birds eating birdseed from the hanging feeders. Every now and then she would notice me outside and would put her paw up against the window as if to say hello. She was there that night, but didn't see me watching her. I smiled, glad to know that she was safe and warm, and wondered if my mother was as well.

My thoughts were interrupted as the cold snow swirled around me mercilessly, and the cold air tickled the ends of my long whiskers as reality whispered its undeniable truths, telling me it was time to leave. I wandered past single family homes; their steaming chimneys announced the warmth I would not have. The air seemed even colder with that thought, and I continued on my way toward the back alley of one of the clothing stores. There I found my soggy cardboard box, curled up as best I could, and tried to sleep. I still remember how the wind howled around me. I was cold, wet, and miserable, and sleep came with difficulty. I didn't think my life could get much worse. And yet, it did.

Chapter 12

The Fire

The intensifying snow squalls made me feel more alone and sad than ever before as each gray, sunless day grew shorter and darker. That's just the nature of things. My daily routine stayed pretty much the same. As the cold weather became more intolerant, it took a concerted effort to find shelter at night and to forage for food during the day. It's difficult to be happy when you have no home and sometimes have very little food to eat. But, thanks to Chester, at least I knew how to find food, although I wasn't always successful, and I knew how to create shelters from the discarded cardboard boxes in back of some of the retail stores. Those makeshift shelters helped protect me from the cold and wind. I even figured out how to position the open end of a box against a wall so the wind didn't blow directly into my shelter.

The last two days of December brought an incessant number of storms and produced the first lasting accumulation of snow. That's when I realized that sometimes things aren't always as you first perceive them to be. The seemingly fragile, frozen ice crystals that fell as beautiful white flakes could turn into heavy, wet harbingers of misery. A large amount of snow would collapse the roof of my fabricated house, and even if my shelter managed to survive the snow load, the cardboard would become so wet and soggy that water would drip onto me all night while I tried to sleep. After several storms, I learned that several inches of snow wasn't always a bad thing, though, because a small amount actually provided a blanket of insulation over the shelter. It helped to keep my body heat within the shelter from leaking out into the cold air.

Snowstorms from the last two days of December continued into the first few days of January. By then, snow had accumulated well over seven feet high in some areas of town. The alleyways near the diner and around the retail stores on the main streets had several feet of snowdrifts as well, and food was scarce and hard to find. Few people were out and about, and I hadn't even seen any of my friends for several days. Since the heavy snowstorms had become continuous events over a four-day period, everyone had stayed in their respective homes.

On the morning of the fifth day into January, the sky turned from endless white clouds to murky gray ones. Rain-swollen stratus clouds turned cold and the continuous light snow changed to sleet, freezing rain, and then back once again to intermittent flakes of fluffy snow. I took the opportunity between the sporadic snow squalls to wander down the alley by the dumpster to check out the food supply. I was hungry. I heard the familiar squeak of the old screen door at the side entrance of the diner just as I rounded the corner to the alley and spotted Harvey as he was throwing out a few pieces of chicken innards from a small platter into the dumpster.

"There you go, rats, eat up while you still can," I heard Harvey say as he looked over his shoulder and walked back toward the side door of the storage shed. "I know there are still some of you around here," he continued with the empty platter hanging from one hand. "Since I've had that black cat around here now, it don't seem like there are so many of you nowadays." He shouted it toward the dumpster.

I laughed to myself at Harvey's comment. If he only knew, I thought, that the awful tasting ketchup was not the real thing. I hadn't helped him out a bit. He still had the same number of rodents he always had. They just hid a little better.

Harvey continued his diatribe in a loud voice as his imaginary conversation continued. "Listen up, you rats, the garbage truck should be here tomorrow to empty this container. I'll take care of you before that, though." His disdain for rats hadn't changed. It never would. "I've got some other treats for you bums later today. Just you wait and see." I watched as Harvey disappeared through the entrance to the shed. I heard the familiar squeak of the screen door, and the inner door slammed shut as I reached the dumpster.

I positioned myself into a crouching position, gathered my energy, and then jumped up and over into the garbage. I hadn't eaten much in several days and, being weak, almost didn't make it over the container's edge. No rats were around, and although there were only a few uncooked scraps of meat that had been thrown away, I ate what there was. The older food scraps appeared unfit to eat. Everything else had spoiled and was starting to smell bad.

Feeling tired and weak, I took a nap on top of some old, empty cardboard food containers and fell asleep for several hours. It was afternoon when I awoke, and the sky was a murky green-gray color like a thickened, spoiled pea soup. The intermittent flakes of fluffy snow from the earlier morning were replaced by persistent heavy, wet ones. I exited the dumpster through one of the jagged holes on one side so I wouldn't have to expend more energy by jumping over the edge once again. I was careful to avoid the sharp edges. Still hungry, I was cold and wet from the fallen snow. As I looked toward the diner, I realized why I hadn't seen any of my dumpster-diving friends. The drainpipe the rats used as a tunnel had water frozen over the top of the pipe, blocking the only entrance. They were stuck inside the storage shed, at least until some of the ice melted from the entrance to the drain.

I left the alley and noticed the sky was quickly changing color from its murky green-gray to a dark, almost black hue. The intensity of the wind had also increased. I knew that the dark clouds overhead meant a large storm was approaching. Both Chester and Buster had taught me that. I just wasn't sure how bad it would be. I didn't have the televised weather reports like people did, so I couldn't prepare in advance for the winter weather. I just knew that the increasing cloud cover, growing darkness, the fact that there were few people about, and that everything was closing up early were ominous signs of things to come.

I decided it might be smarter to try and stay at Buster's place. It would be warm, dry, and safe from the storm. So I figured it was time to visit my friend to see if I could sleep in the basement of the tenement building that night. On my way, I also stopped by Chester's house to see if he was outside, but couldn't find him. I guessed his family wouldn't let him outside and I continued my trek.

The snowfall was several inches deep on the sidewalk and slowed my travel. As I approached Buster's building, my eyes started to water and I could smell the thick, bitter scent of scorched wood. Smoke greeted me like a dense coastal fog as it drifted and flowed over the front stoops of each tenement building. There were two large red fire trucks with ladders and flashing red lights directly in front of Buster's house. Blue flashing lights from two police cruisers also pierced the falling snow, and the mixture of colored lights bestowed a baleful reflection from the solemn faces of concerned neighbors. Tenants had vacated their apartments and stood in the center of the street out of the way of the firefighters. They were wearing heavy winter jackets, trying to stay warm while nervously watching and anxiously waiting to learn the extent of the fire and its consequences to their homes.

Several firefighters attached fire hoses to a nearby fire hydrant at the curb, extending and routing them toward the rear of the building. Shouts from the firemen emanated back and forth from the street to the rear of the building, and as I stood in front of the building, I listened carefully to their frantic conversations.

"It's the rags and a few scraps of framing studs in the basement that are on fire," said one of the firefighters as he came from the rear of the building. "Get those hoses attached to the hydrant and get them into the basement—hurry. We've got to get the fire out before it gets to the stacks of old newspapers down there. It looks like it just started, but if we don't get those hoses into the basement quickly enough, we could have a real problem on our hands."

"Is anyone in the basement?" shouted another firefighter.

"No, we haven't found anyone yet. We're still trying to see through all the smoke."

"Well, make sure. There's too much smoke down there for anyone to survive very long without fresh air."

"I'm going back right now. I just wanted to route a secondary hose down there."

Hearing the conversation, I zigzagged my way across the hoses in front of the building. My worry increased as I inhaled the thick smoke as it crept toward me from the alleyway. I knew there was a chance that Buster might be down in the basement, snuggled into his favorite hidden sleeping spot. No one would ever find him there. If the smoke was too heavy, he could become unconscious and might suffocate. I couldn't allow that to happen to my friend.

I scurried around the crowd of people who had vacated the building and dodged the firemen who were removing equipment from their truck. Then I nimbly jumped over the expanding water hoses that were strewn throughout the alley, followed their path toward the rear of the building, and hurtled through the open bulkhead door and down the stairs into the basement.

"Whoa, where are you going?" shouted one of the firefighters, who was spraying foam over portions of the smoldering rags and lumber as I ran over the toes of his boots. Another firefighter reached down to catch me with one hand while he was trying to hold onto a pressurized fire hose with the other, but he was too late, and I was too quick.

The air was thick with smoke, impairing my vision. Foam and water seemed to be everywhere. My eyes smarted from the fumes, and the acrid taste in my mouth seemed to burn my throat every time I swallowed.

Even though I couldn't see very well, I knew exactly where Buster would be if he had been sleeping in the basement when the fire started. I searched for him, undaunted by my lack of vision and motivated by the need to save my friend. After bumping blindly into boxes and stacks of papers as I tried to avoid pockets of heavy smoke, I finally located the spot where Buster usually slept. The dense man-made fog drifted and swirled around me, limiting my perception of shapes and living things. For one brief moment, however, I was barely able to make out the lifeless image of my large friend lying on his prefabricated bed. He was in the basement after all, but he was motionless.

I jumped up onto the crumpled sheets of his bed and nudged his nose with mine. "Are you okay?" I asked.

There was no response, and his eyes were closed. I could not wake him. Buster's breathing was shallow. I started to panic at the thought of not being able to save him.

"I've got to get you out of here!" I exclaimed loudly to him, hoping he might hear me. Then I thought about the many things I had learned by being on my own for the past several months. I realized that I needed to organize my thoughts and act quickly. I had to remain calm and think things through. That's what I had done when Bracken was in trouble, and it had worked. I couldn't wait for others to act. If I approached the firemen, they wouldn't understand what I was trying to tell them. They would only carry me out of the basement, not understanding there was another cat that needed to be rescued. I was the only one that knew about my friend who was hidden from sight. It was my responsibility alone to find a solution.

Remembering the lesson I had learned the day that Buster had saved the kitten from falling out of the maple tree, I knew what I had to do. I grabbed him by the loose skin on the back of his neck and pulled him off the old sheets he was lying upon.

"You are one heavy cat," I complained loudly as I slid Buster off the sheets and onto the basement floor with all my might. Still, there was no response. "I've got to get you out of this smoke so you can breathe." I wheezed as I spoke, dragging him across the floor and gulping in what small amount of air that was available. "Don't you die on me!" I knew that I had to get Buster to safety and outside the bulk-head to the rear of the building.

Since I could hardly breathe myself, I knew that Buster was in even a worse condition than I was. I didn't know how long he had been unconscious in the dense smoke.

It took all of my remaining strength to drag Buster across the basement floor and over the fire hoses that ran up the stairs through the open bulkhead door to the outside. Sometimes, under adverse conditions, we find an inner strength we don't even know we have. I learned that about myself that night, the fact that I had inner strength—we all do.

As I sat there outside the building, looking at Buster and hoping he'd wake up, I realized the fire had been safely extinguished, and the firemen were removing the hoses that had been channeled through the bulkhead. I was a little groggy from inhaling so much smoke but still understood the loud conversation between two of the firemen who were exiting the building.

"Did you see that black cat dragging that other cat, twice his size, out of the basement?" yelled one firefighter to another.

"Yeah, I never even saw that other cat down there. I looked around, but I missed him. The smoke was just too thick. We caught the fire just in time before it had a chance to spread to the stacks of old newspapers. I'm not sure where that other cat was."

"Yeah, that black cat ran right across my boots. He seemed like he knew exactly where he was going. Why don't you see if you can help that other cat? I don't know if he's dead or alive. Get some oxygen to him."

"Okay, I'm right on it," was the reply. The second firefighter ran out of the basement to one of the fire trucks and quickly grabbed a small canister of oxygen. It was a special device that had a small oxygen mask suited for people's pets such as dogs and cats. He ran back to where I was sitting next to Buster. Then he knelt down next to both of us, attached the mask over Buster's nose, and turned the wheel on the small cylinder to start the oxygen flow.

A few moments later, Buster sleepily opened his eyes. Coughing, he inhaled large portions of the fresh oxygen and woke up slightly dazed. "You'll be all right!" the firefighter exclaimed. "You're one big cat. I'm amazed your buddy here could even move you—probably saved your life."

I was still slightly wobbly from the lack of fresh air, but sat up straight. The firefighter turned to face me and said, "You'd make one heck of a firefighter, you would."

I was still coughing a little, exhaling remnants of smoke, but smiled wryly, gratified by the remark. Buster laid there, just happy to be alive. A special bond formed between us that night, one I'll always cherish. Saving another life—well, that was something very special. During the course of our friendship, Buster had taught me many things so I could take care of myself. But on that night, I learned I could do much more than that. I could also take care of someone else.

As I sat there thinking about what had just happened, I overheard one of the firefighters direct an interesting question to the others. "Do we know what caused the fire?"

Buster was barely able to sit up at that point and still looked a bit unsteady. I'm sure he didn't hear the answer.

"It was a bunch of kids in the neighborhood smoking cigarettes," was the response. "One of the first police responders caught one of them leaving the premises, and he squealed on the others. Evidently, they didn't extinguish one of their cigarettes properly. Wait till their parents are notified! They won't be happy about this at all, and those kids won't be thinking about smoking in the near future, at least not in the basement of this house. Luckily, the smoke detectors sent an alarm to the fire station. Good thing they're a code requirement. Otherwise, the entire building could have gone up in flames. As a result of the quick alarm response, no one was hurt, not even that cat over there, thanks to his buddy. If that black cat hadn't been so intent on barging his way into the basement, running over our hoses and our boots and ignoring our shouts, we never would have known there was a cat in there that needed help." Pointing at Buster, he then said, "Whose cat is that anyway?"

"I'll take care of him," was a curt and quick shout from the alleyway. I looked up at the outburst and was surprised to see it was Jessie. Once I had overheard that a bunch of kids had been smoking cigarettes in the basement, I knew who they were talking about and figured Jessie, Jason, and Jake were in real trouble with the police, the fire department, and their parents.

"My mom's gonna be really mad at me about those cigarettes," Jessie lamented to the firefighter. "The least I can do is watch the cat tonight and make sure he's all right. I'll take him back home with me." And with that comment, he picked Buster up, gave me a grateful wink, and timidly walked back toward the front entrance of the tenement building, knowing he was in real trouble.

The fire and police departments completed their checks of the area to ensure there were no additional threats of fire and, before leaving, they closed up the bulkhead so no one could enter. By the time they left the building, the storm had changed from a freezing rain to hail and then back to sleet. Still slightly disoriented, I stood up and searched the darkness surrounding me. There were no flashing lights. The fire trucks and police cars were gone. I looked down at the empty spot where I had dragged Buster, and with a slight wheeze to my breathing, realized I was alone.

The night was suddenly quiet except for the sound of sleet tapping against the nearby windowpanes—a storm's foreboding, warning me of its approach. Everyone else had returned to the warmth of their homes. Everyone that was...except for me.

Chapter 13

The Storm and the Trap

The wind roared down the alley like an oncoming freight train, and the cold, driving sleet that followed reminded me it was time to find shelter from the storm. I checked the entrance to the basement, but even the small openings in the side of the bulkhead had been blocked by metal trash cans. There was no entry. The fire department had boarded over the top of the bulkhead in order to prevent snow and water from entering the basement. My idea to stay with Buster didn't quite work out the way I had hoped it would.

I was cold and completely soaked from all the water sprayed throughout the basement while the firemen had tried to contain the spread of the fire. None of my alternative sleeping accommodations were available. I was out of options, and I knew I'd have to weather the storm in my soggy, cardboard shelter. What I didn't know at the time was that the storm was to be the first blizzard of the winter. That meant the winds would circle in from the ocean with increased force, visibility would deteriorate, making it difficult to see more than two feet in front of my face, and there would be more snow in one storm than I had ever experienced.

As I left the alley alongside the brick tenement building, I realized the air had gotten much colder. Perhaps it seemed that way due to the funnel-like effect of the alleyway that caused an increase in the velocity of the wind against my wet fur. Within minutes, dusk had turned into night, and the sleet had once again turned into a heavy, wet snow. Street lamps sparsely positioned along the sidewalks provided the only light available, casting a dim, ghostly glow, and visibility was impeded by the smothered effects of drifting snow, pursued by a never-ending wind.

I started to wander back to my cardboard home with the thought of finding some sort of shelter no matter whether it was soggy or not. I believed it was the only alternative I had and figured it would at least be warmer and drier than staying out in an open alleyway. It would have been so much better if I could have gotten Harvey's attention before he had gone back into the diner earlier that day. He might have put me back in the shed to "catch" more rats. Just thinking about that fallacy brought a knowing smile to my face as I trudged through the ever-increasing depth of snow. I had never caught any of his rats, nor would I ever.

Just as I got to the alley in back of the clothing store, I saw Tate in his familiar tattered coat walking away from me, down the alley with several cardboard boxes folded underneath his arm. His decomposing shoes were filled with snow from drifts he tried to avoid that had reached to just below his knees. Except for all that snow, the alleyway was empty. My cardboard condo house was gone, and there were no other boxes left.

The old man had taken everything for himself. He, too, was looking for something to shelter himself from the blizzard. Sometimes, the actions you take can adversely affect those around you without even realizing it. You can't always foretell what consequences those actions will have on others. The old man didn't know he had taken my only shelter. I believe he would have left one of the boxes had he known I needed one. All that I ever knew about him was that he wasn't a cruel person, only homeless. He never spoke to anyone. For years, he had nothing to say. His actions, however, had a direct effect on my life that night.

"Now what am I going to do?" I lamented to myself. My outcry went unnoticed, leaving only loneliness and despair. As I exhaled, I could see the warm vapor of that question disappear into the night air. I knew that I had to get out of the storm or I would freeze to death.

I sludged my way down the alley through the mounting snowdrifts and tried to catch up to Tate as he disappeared around the corner. I could barely see ahead as I tried to follow his footprints as best I could, hoping he would share the cardboard he had taken. But as he crossed the street far ahead of me, he dissolved into the darkness. By then it was snowing so hard that I could hardly see two feet in front of my nose. With the help of the dimly-lit street lamps, I was barely able to follow the sidewalk.

Desperation set in as I realized I had no cardboard shelter to go to. Tate had removed everything. I was frantic and knew I had to find something. I was still drenched from the water hosed onto the fire, and the freezing temperatures had frozen my long fur into stiff, sharp needles, making it difficult to walk. The unkind wind was so strong I could hardly catch my breath as it forced more air into me than I could expel.

My options for any kind of shelter had dwindled to none at all, and I wandered from door to door. I searched for anything that could provide some sort of protection from the weather, but everything was locked up tight. People had prepared for the big storm and had made sure doors to storage sheds, garages, and basements were all secured. The drifting snow was so deep that it made it impossible to even approach some areas, and as I continued my search, darkness made it increasingly difficult to find my way.

The cold climbed out of the ground and into my feet as I wandered. My long whiskers drooped from the cold ice that also formed around my once pink nose that I'm sure seemed to turn almost blue in color from the freezing air. My eyes watered from the fierce, cold wind and teared from the freezing air, causing my eyelids to stick together as I blinked. Breathing became increasingly more difficult as the wind attacked my chest with ferocity. It felt like my heart would explode.

Exhausted, I found myself facing the front door to the diner. It was closed just like everything else. No lights were on, not even the neon sign above the entrance. A clear single thought entered my mind as I remembered a comment that Harvey had made earlier that morning. I had overheard him say, "I've got some other treats for you bums later today. Just wait, you'll see." It made me wonder if Harvey had thrown some food into the dumpster that afternoon like he said he was going to do. If he had, I could at least get something to eat. Perhaps the dumpster would also provide a little shelter.

With a decided shove from an insistent wind, I decided to check out the dumpster. The snow fell fast, thick, and heavy, and wrapped my fur with a white crust. I meandered blindly down the alley, fighting the force of the howling wind with every step, and finally stumbled into the side of the old dumpster. Looking up, I found that the lid of the dumpster had been left open. Harvey had forgotten to close it again, even with a storm coming. With little strength remaining, I crouched, then jumped over the high steel wall as I had done so on many other occasions. I fell upright on all four feet directly into the garbage below.

At the very instant I landed on top of the garbage, however, I heard a loud snap and felt the burning slash of sharp steel that cut through fur and flesh. Chiseled jaws of a leghold trap sprang tightly shut, cutting into my left front paw. With excruciating pain, I fell over onto my side. The raging blizzard swallowed the sounds of my cries of fear and pain. There was no one to hear me. I could barely see anything in the dimly lit alley. The large snowflakes reflected an eerie light from the dim street lamp at the end of the alley. It was as if I was in a dream. I could barely see anything surrounding me. I couldn't even see my paw, but I could feel the warmth of the blood as it trickled down my foot. The sharp pain was unbearable. It was then that I thought I might die, and memories of my short life flooded my thoughts—my mother, my siblings, my new friends, my father, my unanswered questions, my bitterness—all at the same time.

There comes a time when you don't think you can move on, and you actually wonder if you should. Then you think of the things you want to do and the things you haven't seen or done yet, and there's a will to go on. That's what I thought about in those fleeting moments. It happens to people as well as animals. There's an inner voice in all of us that says, "Don't give up. Keep trying." And so, you do. I did. I had that fierce will to live. It wasn't a matter of courage, but an inability to let go.

Part II

Then and Now

Chapter 14

Survival

-The Present

I wake abruptly as the open lid of the dumpster reflects the first rays of the morning sunlight onto the side of my face. Startled, I sense relief from an unending night of darkness as morning intervenes. The wet chill from the night's howling wind has frozen droplets of water on my eyes into tiny icicles that have begun to melt. My eyelids refuse to fully open, allowing only a glimpse of the sun as it peers through the clouds that scatter the sky like hope clings to possibilities. Drifting snow from the relentless wind during the night partially covers me and presses hard against my long black fur like a cold blanket that surrounds my body. I still find it difficult to breathe. I think it's ironic that the snow itself has insulated me from the wind chill and the blizzard now past—perhaps that's why I'm still alive. The snow has risen all around me as if I'm at the bottom of a crevasse.

Even though I can't see very well, I can hear the faint warmth of the sun approach as ice crystals expand and crackle into subsets of their former selves. Snowmelt trickles from above, and small beads of water form as frozen whiskers flat against my face are released from their deep sleep. I am exhausted.

Random images creep throughout my clouded thoughts, and pain and hunger hamper my ability to focus on my surroundings. A soft whisper emanates from the depths of past memories—a voice, strong and deep—from a dark figure that once again lingers, looking down at me, calling my name, and I fall back into unconsciousness.

Hours drip past, and I feel a nudge at my shoulder.

"Hey you, Patches."

The abrupt declaration disturbs my fettered conscious-
ness and wakes me from my fitful sleep. I am acutely aware
of the excruciating pain from my partially severed paw and
the reality of my injury. My foot is cold. I try to stretch and
sense that blood has dried around my toes. My foot is heavy
from the added weight of the trap, and the sharp, steel jaws
remain clamped tightly around my paw. I can't feel my toes.
I'm not sure if it's because of the cold or because of the se-
verity of my injury. I try to lift my head and face the sound
of the familiar voice, but my efforts are in vain. I am too
weak. The morning sun, however, has now melted the ice
crystals from my eyelids, and I can peer through those shallow slits and try to adjust my blurred vision.

The voice startles me once again and repeats my name.
"You don't look so good."

I recognize the 1930s mobster-like accent and know it's
Amos even without being able to see the details of his image.

He speaks again. "I think that trap was meant for us rats,
not you. That Harvey Stunk really doesn't like us, nor anyone
else for that matter. I think he was trying to get even with us
for messing up his kitchen with the health inspector and all
those other pranks we've pulled on him."

I sense that Amos keeps looking at my paw. I can barely
see the concern on his face—sharp, pointed whiskers and all.
His voice sounds noticeably upset as he speaks once again.
"Those steel-jaw leg-hold traps are inhumane! They should
be outlawed!" The tone of his voice makes me worried.

I'm lying on a pile of garbage and listening to Amos as he
continues to curse the use of traps. I open my eyes wider. I
can see Ollie and Olive looking at my foot as well. Their combined expressions reinforce my fear that, somehow, I am in
real trouble—especially when they mimic their brother's
comments and agree with his perception on the use of traps.

Ollie approaches my foot, sniffing the trap and pawing at
its hinge, sticking his pointed nose close to the sharp edges
of steel. After a hurried observation, he exclaims, "We have
to help him! Let's see if we can gnaw the side of the trap to
open it."

"Okay," replies Olive. "It's a good thing we were able to chew a hole in the ice at the end of the drainpipe. Otherwise, we'd still be stranded in the storage shed and wouldn't be out here to help."

Brother and sister get on each side of the trap while Amos continues to assess my plight and tries to think of anything else they can possibly do. Each of them tries chewing the steel hinges, but the metal is just too hard, even for their sharp teeth. All they manage to do is to scratch the hard surface, leaving long, thin scratch marks across the metal.

"It's not like those tin cans we can sometimes chew open," remarks Ollie as he suddenly chips one of his front teeth. I see that he's upset and frustrated with his failed attempt, not even caring about his jagged tooth. "We can't chew through this metal. It's just too hard."

They try pulling back on the top of the trap, but no matter how hard they try, they can't get the jaws to open. "What can we do?" Ollie and Olive both question Amos in unison. They are visibly upset over their failure to remove the trap. So am I.

I can't think of anything my friends can do to help me. And the morning quiet ends when I hear the sound of a garbage truck as it rounds the corner of the alley. It barrels through the snow and comes to a screeching halt next to the dumpster. Steam rises from the hood of the truck as remaining layers of snow begin to melt from the heat of the engine. We all realize the garbage truck has arrived, and the dumpster will be emptied.

Amos speaks first. "We need to do something quickly. If that garbage truck picks this dumpster up and empties it, we can scurry out, but Patches can't. He's got the jaws of that trap clamped right around his paw, and he can't move. He'll be crushed by all the garbage!"

"Maybe if we make a lot of noise, the truck driver will look in here and see him!" Ollie exclaims. "Then we can jump out before the garbage is dumped so we don't get caught as well."

"Yeah, that's a good idea," Amos replies. "We need to do something quick. That nasty leg trap was meant for us. We just can't let him suffer, or worse yet, die because of that trap embedded in his foot. It just wouldn't be right. He's been a good friend, even though he is a cat."

I don't take any offense to Amos' last comment because I know he is trying to relieve the tension from their unsuccessful attempts to help. It even brings a thoughtful smile knowing I have friends with me and they are trying to help.

All three rats start to squeal. Shrill noises resonate throughout the metal walls of the dumpster. Ollie and Olive scamper through the paper and old food wrappers that make loud crinkling sounds. Empty tin cans rattle against the side of the dumpster, and Amos manages to make even more noise by pushing empty glass bottles into one another so they crash against the metal container walls.

There are two people in the garbage truck. Mick is the driver and older than his younger assistant, Mack, whose job it is to attach the dumpsters to the truck so they can be lifted and emptied. Even with all the noise created by my friends, I can hear the beeping sound of the heavy garbage truck as it backs up closer to the dumpster, and the ice moans and crackles under its tires. It comes to a stop and I can hear the muffled sound of two distinct voices.

Mick rolls the window down on the driver's side of the truck to get a better view of its proximity to the dumpster. "I think we're close enough," he says to Mack as he peers out the side window, looking toward the rear of the truck.

Mack rolls his window down as well and fully extends his head out the window, looking to see if Mick has lined up the truck for the pickup. "Looks good," he says. "I'll get out and latch the dumpster."

"When you're ready, I'll turn on the trash compactor once you've emptied the garbage into the truck," Mick replies. "That'll compress the trash from the last two loads we picked up."

The rats are busy making as much noise as they can. It sounds like two armies raging a battle inside the dumpster. The commotion they make causes a deafening sound and is further amplified by the reverberation from the steel walls. Over the chaotic sounds, Amos scampers over to me and whispers in my ear, "Hang in there, we're gonna get you out of this mess—somehow."

Evidently, the noise created by my friends is loud enough to catch Mick's attention as he backs up the truck. "What's all the racket?" he asks Mack. "Take a look inside that garbage bin before you latch it and see what's going on in there. It sounds like a lot of rodents scampering about, and I don't want to dump them into the back of our truck. One thing we don't need is more rats in the town dump."

"Okay, I'll check inside before I latch it for dumping," Mack replies as he steps out and walks toward the rear of the truck. He stands in front of the dumpster and cautiously peers over the edge into the container. "Looks like Harvey left the lid open again," he shouts. "There's a ton of snow in here from last night's blizzard."

As soon as Amos and his siblings see Mack peeking over the edge, they quickly retreat under some empty soup cans and hide from sight. Lying on the top of the garbage, partially covered by melting snow, Mack sees me. I sense his presence and lift my head slightly when I hear his voice. He notices the dried blood that covers my front paw. A shiny glint of sunshine catches his eye and exposes the ugly steel teeth of the trap, partially hidden underneath the wet rubbish.

"Hey, Mick," yells Mack. "There's a cat in here. His front foot has been caught by one of those steel animal traps. It looks pretty bad."

"What blooming idiot would put a trap in the dumpster?" Mick exclaims as he steps out of the truck to see what Mack is talking about. There is a sense of anguish in his voice, causing me to think he's upset because he might be a real animal lover. "Is he still alive?"

"Yeah, but his paw looks like it's cut pretty badly," replies Mack. "It must have been Harvey trying to catch rats again. You know how he is. We've both told him time and time again not to do this. The trap's imbedded in the cat's foot. He's in pretty bad shape, and it looks like he's lost a bit of blood. He may have been in some sort of fire as well. Some of his fur is singed and crusted at the ends. I'd say that this poor guy has recently had a few bad days, especially last night. He also looks malnourished. I can see the outlines of his ribs. I wonder when he ate last? There certainly isn't much in this container that's edible. It smells pretty bad."

"We need to get him to an animal shelter or someplace where's there's a veterinarian," replies Mick. "We can't just leave him here. He'll die."

Mack looks down at me and I can see from the expression on his face that he understands I am in a real state of distress. I can hear Mick's footsteps as he quickly walks over to the dumpster in order to help. Being the good Samaritans they are, they both gently lift me like a limp dishrag from the garbage, trap and all, carry me back to the garbage truck, and place me between them on an old blanket in the front seat. The heat in the cab from the engine enlivens me.

"There's an animal shelter in the next town, not far from here. We adopted a dog from them last year," Mick says. "They might have a vet on duty."

"Let's go. We can empty the remaining garbage bins later today," replies Mack.

There's a grinding sound of metal upon metal as the old truck shifts into first gear and speeds off over the newly formed ice, through the high snowdrifts, down the alley, and onto the main road toward the animal shelter.

The ride is uncomfortable as the big, old garbage truck bounces over potholes and lumbers through the hard, crusted ice drifts that remain from last night's storm. My paramedical trip to the animal shelter is like a fleeting moment in my life. I whisper their names to myself—Mick and Mack. I don't want to forget their names. I hear their voices. I feel their kindness. I absorb the warmth of the old blanket that covers me from head to toe. I can smell the stink of diesel fuel and hear the creaking sounds of the old truck that simply refuses to let the condition of any snowy road stop its rescue mission. Sights and sounds fade once again.

I wake to an intense white light shining in my face. I feel like a melted snowman as I lay on a metal table. The old blanket is still beneath me. I can still smell the diesel fuel. I open my eyes and see a tall, lanky man in a very long white coat examining my left front paw. The sharp steel teeth of the trap are no longer embedded across my toes. The trap is gone, but I still feel pain.

Dr. Vincent Roberts is the shelter's veterinarian. He helps out two days a week and volunteers his time to treat diseased and injured animals. He performs surgery, sets broken bones, and prescribes medications to the animals as needed. His assistant's name is Kelly Breen. She is studying to be a medical technician at a nearby college and has just started working at the shelter on a full-time basis.

I watch him examine my paw, wonder what will happen next, and keep quiet.

"What's the story with this cat?" Kelly asks as she enters the examining room where Dr. Roberts has been looking over my injuries. I pay close attention to what they are doing and carefully listen to their conversation.

"Two sanitation workers brought him in a few minutes ago. They found him in a dumpster. Medically speaking, he's a very emaciated long-haired young adult male with a badly injured front paw. A steel-jaw leg hold trap was sprung on his paw, causing the injury to his foot. It was difficult to take the trap off without causing more injury, but I managed to remove it. His foot is swollen and the skin is badly cut on the front of his paw. It looks like the paw might have to be removed."

I wince at the assessment and prognosis.

"Is there anything we can do in order to save the paw?" asks Kelly.

"I'm not sure. That's what I'm trying to decide. The trap cut across his dew claw and one toe. Most cats have four toes on their paws and an extra toe up higher than the other toes, something like a human thumb, called a dew claw. I don't think I can save all of his toes, but I may be able to save the rest of the foot," replies Roberts. "I'll know better when I get an x-ray. Once we do that, we can get him ready for surgery and do the best we can for him. We don't know anything about his overall health, so we'll just have to take a chance on his recovery. It's better than not doing anything at all."

I'm terrified of losing my left front paw. It also doesn't help that I'm alone once again in an unfamiliar place. All the strange-looking medical equipment adds to my fears of what might happen next. I look up to see a small mask being placed over my nose. It reminds me of the oxygen mask the firefighters used for Buster, except this apparently isn't just oxygen. It seems to be a balanced dose of oxygen and something to make me sleepy. They are going to operate on my foot—now.

The fear of the unknown can be the worst type of fear. I worry about the possibilities of losing my paw or not waking up at all. I feel tired and the pain subsides as I drift in and out of unconsciousness and dream once again.

Chapter 15

Discovery

-The Past

Not long after they were first married, Abigail and Sam Howard noticed an ad in the classified section of their local newspaper. It read, "Kittens for Sale." The ad represented a breeding cattery where pedigree show cats were bred and raised for sale. That's where they found a cat they named Mittens. She was a small long-haired cat, and, at most, weighed about seven pounds. She had black fur, a long white patch of fur on her chest, a white patch from her forehead down on both sides of her pink nose, and white paws. Sounds a little familiar, doesn't it?

The woman who owned the cattery was a real snob about the pedigree of the cats she sold and had no record of Mittens' ancestry. Mittens was considered to be a small Ragdoll cat and happened to be the only one at the cattery like her. That's because she wasn't a pure bred and just didn't fit the type of pedigree the woman normally sold.

Sam and Abby decided to visit the cattery, look at what they had, and perhaps purchase a kitten to add a little character to their new and somewhat quiet household.

The cattery consisted of three large rooms in an old, privately owned house. One room contained several kittens running about and playing. The owner told Sam and Abby to look around and see if they wanted to purchase any of them. That's when they noticed Mittens playing all by herself in one corner of the room, aloof from all noises and interactions of the other cats. As they continued to look about the room of playful kittens, the woman noticed their interest.

Pointing at Mittens, she said, "She doesn't have a pedigree like the others. You can have her real cheap."

Sam and Abby didn't care so much about the cost. They just wanted a kitten—well, at first, maybe Abby more than Sam. But they left the cattery that morning without the kitten. It seemed as though Sam was under the impression they were only going to look at kittens—not look and buy immediately, a grave misunderstanding on Sam's part. So, after they got home and discussed the difference, Sam got to understand what the word "look" really meant, and he was smart enough to go back that same afternoon and purchase the kitten for Abby. It was the ride home that convinced Sam this had been the right choice because the kitten meowed the entire way home, climbing over the top of his seat, sitting on his shoulders, and looking through the driver's side window as he tried to drive. It was a trip he never forgot.

Once they had a cat, it didn't take Sam very long to recognize and to later understand the important relationship between people and family pets. Mittens thrived on human companionship and devoted herself entirely to Sam and Abby, especially Abby. She loved to be held and cuddled. She brought happiness and, of course, a lot of character to their home.

Several years after getting Mittens, they also provided a home to an abandoned German Shepherd they named Heidi. One of the secretaries where Sam worked brought the dog into the office to see if anyone would give her a home. She had discovered her in their barn, all alone, dying from starvation. Upon seeing the homeless black and white dog, Sam made the comment that he had always wanted a German Shepherd. He didn't say he wanted to adopt the dog, only that he had always wanted one. Much to his disbelief, though, the secretary immediately called Abigail and told her Sam wanted the dog.

"Not so," said Sam, but no one ever believed him.

And so, with Abby's empathy toward the dog's situation, and Mittens' final approval, the dog got a permanent home. The unlikely pair of dog and cat became very good friends over the years—one very large dog and one very small cat—and over time, they both played a large part in bringing up Sam and Abby's two sons.

Mittens was always an indoor cat, and they never let her outside on her own. There were predators like foxes and coyotes, as well as hawks and owls that lived in the forest around their home, and she was safer and healthier staying inside. The things she missed from not being allowed to roam outside included getting lost, getting hit by a car, exposure to disease and fleas, attacks by dogs, eating something that shouldn't be eaten, and even being injured by steel-jaw traps, just to name a few. There were just too many risks.

Mittens lived with Sam and Abby for almost twenty years. She wasn't like most other cats, at least not in Sam's and Abby's eyes. Every animal has a distinct personality, and Mittens certainly was a distinctive addition to the family. She was a constant companion to Abby, who had the full-time job of raising their two boys and taking care of all the household duties. She slept with Sam and Abby, along with the dog in a king-sized bed every night and never left Abby's side.

Mittens always brought warmth and character to their home, and when she passed away on an early spring morning, five years after Heidi had passed away, there was a deep sorrow and strange emptiness.

It was her passing that prompted Sam and Abby to build a solarium attached to their house. It took them all summer to build it. Sam built a cement block wall foundation and used stone dust as a base. He used loose bricks, placed slightly apart from each other, to make up the floor. They hung the joists, extended a roof from the second floor of the house, added five skylights, three of which could be opened for ventilation, and attached a digital thermometer so they could compare inside and outside temperatures. It had five large panes of glass that extended from the floor to the ceiling, facing the south side of the house, with a screened door that led outside to a small man-made pond with a waterfall that was powered by a utility pump. During sunny days, there was so much light in the room that it felt like you were outside the house, and the added sound of splashing water from the small waterfall enhanced that feeling. They finished construction in early September, just about the same time that Patches found himself homeless.

"Mittens would have liked this room. It looks like you're outdoors, yet you're still safe inside," Sam said to Abby. "We did a pretty good job. I wish we had built this earlier so she could have enjoyed it."

"I do too," replied Abby. "I really miss her."

November approached, and winter in the northeast was one of those inconsistent yet inevitable constants that occurs during the earth's journey around the sun. The days of less sunshine made the house seem empty without Mittens and Heidi. Even their two sons, who were ages nine and eleven at the time, noticed the void. It was then that they decided it was time to adopt a couple of shelter kittens. The house was just too empty, and the newly constructed solarium was built for everyone to use—people and pets alike.

Sam and Abby lived in a coastal town that was on the border of two states, and there were two animal shelters in their local area. One was in New Hampshire and the other one was in Maine. Both were somewhat equidistant from their home. So they called both animal shelters to ask about the availability of long-haired kittens for adoption—they just happened to have a preference for long-haired cats.

On one afternoon in the month of November, which was the same month that Patches had recognized his first fears about surviving a first winter on his own, Abby decided it was time to visit the closest animal shelter. It was only a half-hour away, just a little north of their home in Maine.

The staff at the Maine animal shelter was very accommodating and showed Abby several kittens that afternoon. Kelly, the associate medical technician, took the time to show Abby some of the kittens they had available for adoption.

"We have several rows of cages stacked two high with kittens that vary in age and size, but right now we have fewer kittens than we had a month ago," Kelly informed Abby. "Currently, we have about twelve kittens available and twenty-one older adult cats. We have waived the adoption fees for cats older than eight years. It's simply harder to place them in homes. Now these guys over here in this larger cage are from one litter of four kittens. The mother's name is Jenna. There is one calico multicolored kitten with patches of black, white, and orange-cream colors that looks like her mother and three orange and white kittens, all female. We have the mother cat here with all of them for adoption as well. Hopefully, someone will adopt the mother with one or two of her kittens together. Unfortunately, it's difficult to get someone to adopt an entire family. We don't like to split them up, but usually we don't have a choice. Over here, we have another mother cat with one female kitten. The mother's name is Willow. She had two kittens, and one of them was adopted last week. As you can see, both she and her kitten are a tortoiseshell color. These cages contain all long hair cats. There are three other cages in this aisle that have a couple of kittens each. Some are considered to be medium hair and some short hair. Most of the kittens are around eight weeks old. And don't forget to look at the adult cats as well as the kittens in the next aisle across from these cages. They could use a good home too. The tags on the cages identify the conditions and circumstances of how they arrived here as best that we can determine. So take your time, look around, and let me know if I can help you in any way."

"Thanks, I'll look around," Abby replied as she started to walk slowly by the cages that lined both sides of the wide hallway. While looking, Abby kept in mind that it would be best to adopt two kittens at the same time so they might play together and keep each other company. Abby immediately liked the coloring of the tortoiseshell kitten. She was very petite with speckled patches of black, chocolate, and cinnamon colors. Her sister had already been adopted, and she was the only one left with her mother, Willow.

Abby looked at all the kittens and read the limited information posted on their cages. After an hour of looking at all of them, she called Kelly over with her decision to adopt one of the kittens.

"I'll adopt the one who is all by herself," she said, and pointed to the tortoiseshell kitten. "I want to adopt two kittens, but I'm not sure which other one I want." She looked back into the cage containing the three kittens with their mother, Jenna, while she spoke. That's when Abby noticed a lonely calico kitten in the corner of the cage. She was standing in some cat litter all by herself. Being alone certainly made her stand out from all the other kittens. Abby couldn't keep a straight face and, with a noticeable grin, pointed to the lonely kitten and said to Kelly, "When she's done taking a poop, I'll take that one also."

Sam got home from work late that day to find two very small kittens climbing all over the back of their youngest son, who was lying face-down on their sofa. They were having a grand time running back and forth. Their short, triangular tails stood straight up while they scampered over their new playground, and they looked like little exclamation marks as they played! They named the tortoiseshell kitten Wickett, and the calico kitten Kali.

Both Wickett and Kali were quick learners. Together, they explored all the rooms in their new home, both upstairs and downstairs, and more importantly, discovered cat toys, especially the ones that contained a little catnip. They learned to scratch on a tall scratch post wound with sisal rope that had four carpeted shelving levels on which they could sleep.

The cat post faced an exterior French door that looked out onto several birdfeeders that were hung from an overhead deck that was attached to the second floor of the house. Sam had built the scratch post for them as well as for himself. No—he didn't need it to scratch upon, but it was much better to have the cats use the scratch post rather than to have them use the grill coverings on his stereo speakers. And, besides, the cats enjoyed watching the birds from their elevated perches. They also learned how to get a drink of water out of the sink faucets if they didn't want to drink from their water dishes on the floor. Most importantly, they learned how to use their litter boxes.

Wickett decided to sleep beside Abby every night, which made Abby happy, and Kali decided it was her job to sleep in the hallway and greet anyone that came to the front door. Neither one of the cats was shown the solarium, however, because it was too cold in the season to open it up to the house. Since the room was heated only by the sun, there wasn't sufficient sunshine to heat the solarium up to room temperature during the winter months. Leaving it open to the inside of the house would only cool the house down. When temperatures increased so they could open it up to help heat the house, Sam and Abby thought it would be a great surprise for the cats in the spring.

The months of November and December went by quickly

as the kittens settled into their new home and experienced their first holidays of Thanksgiving and Christmas with their new family. Kali even managed to climb most of the way to the top of her first Christmas tree before getting into difficulty and loudly requesting assistance to get down. Both kittens brought a lot of character to the home.

It was early January when Abby saw the severe weather alert warning on television. "The weather channel says there's a blizzard coming," she commented to Sam. "I'm glad our cats aren't going to be outside. It would be horrible for anyone to be out in it."

"I can't even begin to imagine how animals can survive outside in those conditions," replied Sam. "But I know some do."

The storm started early the next morning as a freezing rain and then turned to heavy, wet snow later in the afternoon. The blizzard continued all night into the early hours of the following morning before sunrise.

"We've got snow drifts almost three feet high in some places," Sam complained as he donned his winter boots, coat, hat, and gloves. "I've got to plow out the driveway before I can get over to the office." Snowstorms continued throughout the rest of January, but none of them were as severe as the northeaster they experienced that day in early January.

It was later in that month when Sam and Abby received a newsletter from the animal shelter in Maine. It was mailed to all who had adopted animals or donated money or food, in hopes the shelter would place more animals in homes. Almost three months had passed since they had adopted Wickett and Kali.

Abby saw the newsletter first and passed it to Sam when he arrived home from work. "Take a look at the second page," she said to Sam.

There was a picture of Patches with a story about his injured paw, the trap, and how he came to the shelter. The article mentioned that he would be up for adoption, but it didn't contain any information about the condition of his paw and whether or not it had been saved. It simply showed his picture with a name the shelter had given him. They called him Figaro, apparently because he looked like a cat from a popular animated children's movie.

The phone number of the animal shelter and a brief script were also included. It read:

"He purrs like crazy when you talk to him or take him out of the cage for a while and hold him. He eats everything offered to him and he is just beginning to gain some weight. He's got no identification and no one has reported him missing so we can't notify his owner. IF HE IS YOUR CAT, PLEASE CALL US. HE WOULD LIKE TO GO HOME. IF YOU WOULD LIKE TO ADOPT HIM, PLEASE CALL THE SHELTER."

"He looks just like—"

"Mittens," interrupted Abby. She had known exactly what Sam was going to say. "The similarity is remarkable. What do you think? Another cat?"

"Looks like it. He kind of pulls on your heartstrings, doesn't he? Go ahead. Why don't you give them a call?"

"What if he's lost his paw?"

"Well, it doesn't really matter, does it? Either way, we'll be able to give him a good home. If we decide to adopt him, however, we've got to remember one thing. Just because he looks like Mittens doesn't mean he'll act like Mittens. You know as well as I do that, in many ways, they're like people. They're all individuals. We both know that. Mittens had a very unique temperament. For instance, I remember when we first built the house, and I came home early from work one day, and you weren't home. I had only one key to the back bedroom sliding door and didn't have a key for the front door. I unlocked that slider in order to get into the house, and I heard Heidi growl from the living room at the other end of the house. I remember thinking, 'this is great, we have a real watch dog.' So I decided to growl back, and then I heard nothing. I growled again, heard some sort of movement in the living room, and then silence once again. As I entered the bedroom from the outside, I heard a loud thumping noise coming from the attached hallway to the bedroom. It sound-ed like someone putting a heavy foot down, one in front of another. I couldn't quite figure out what it was. And into the bedroom trotted Mittens, one heavy foot in front of her at a time. She must have focused all her weight with each step she took in order to make her sound heavier and larger than she was. Even her coat of fur was bristled straight up so she looked to be twice her size. I assumed she did that in order to intimidate the intruder, which in that case, was me. Once she recognized who I was, her fur immediately lowered to her normal small size, and she looked at me as if to say, 'okay, why did you scare my dog?' She then turned and walked back down the hallway. I remember finding Heidi hid-ing behind a chair in the living room, and thought, 'great, we've got a watch cat.'"

Abby smiled at the thought of her tiny cat protecting the dog from any intruder and replied, "She certainly was one of a kind, wasn't she?"

"She sure was," replied Sam. "So, what do you want to do?"

Abby didn't hesitate. She called the shelter and asked, "Is

the cat with the injured paw that you show in your recent newsletter still up for adoption? The shelter calls him Figaro."

"Hold on a minute. I know which cat you're talking about. Let me get his records," was the reply.

Abby could hear a filing cabinet being opened and the shuffling of papers in the background.

"Yes. He's still available. No one has called. There are a lot of people who either can't or don't want to deal with injured pets. This paperwork indicates that his earliest release date would be in six to eight weeks. Apparently, he had some major surgery performed, and we can't let him go until he's healed."

"That's all right. We don't care. We just want to adopt him."

"Have you adopted from us before?"

"Yes, about three months ago. We got two kittens from you."

"Great, all I need is your name and address then, and I'll take care of the paperwork. Anything else I need should be on file. Just call in about six weeks, and I'll give you a status on his condition and an idea of when you can pick him up and take him home. I'll list him as being adopted."

"Thank you. Just one more thing. Were you able to save his paw?"

Part III

Revelations

Chapter 16

Shelter Cats

I wake to the fearsome dream of freezing cold, howling wind, and never-ending snowfall. Daylight from a nearby window eclipses my fear of the long, cold night. I instinctively try to raise my injured foot. It's heavy—just too heavy to lift. Still groggy from the anesthetic, images aren't clear. Without being able to focus my vision, the room is a composition of blurs and colors that seem to dance around me. I have survived the storm, and I am alive—that much I know. My fear prior to surgery of not waking up at all is dispelled. My front left foot aches, but the unbearable pain is gone. And with that realization, I panic as I think about my second worse fear. Do I still have a left front paw?

I'm barely able to raise my head and look around the room. My head feels like a lead anchor. Thoughts race through my mind as past events trip over one another in rapid succession. I remember lying in the dumpster and hearing the strange and unfamiliar voices of two men as they had lifted me out of the garbage. In particular, I remember Amos' voice and his words: "Hang in there, Patches, we're here for you." Memories of the storm, the fire, the cold, and the constant hunger pass by like slow-moving clouds. These seconds of self-reflection seem like hours. I'm still weak, exhausted, and sleepy.

Several hours drift by and I wake hearing voices. Are they part of a dream or are they real? With willful effort, I can now raise my head and look about the room. I see a tall, lanky man in a long white coat. He wasn't a dream after all.

He's real.

"Put Figaro in with the other cats, but only in a cage by himself. He needs to heal," the veterinarian tells his assistant. "We'll take the cast off his foot next week and possibly re-cast it, after we check to make sure it's healing properly."

Who's Figaro? I think, and that's when I understand. Evidently, Figaro is my new name. Since I have no way of telling them my real name, I'll have to accept the new one. I'll have to get used to everyone calling me Figaro from now on. I guess that might not be so bad—at least I'm still here.

I listen carefully to their conversation. The words "check the foot" and "healing properly" are a relief for me to hear. Looking down at my foot as my vision clears, I realize that I still have a paw. I can see the cast that covers a portion of my leg and part of my foot. I understand now why my foot is so heavy to lift.

"I'm so glad you were able to save his paw," Kelly says as she carefully picks me up, paying particular attention to the cast on my leg, and lays me in a large cage.

"I had to amputate a toe and a dew claw, but we saved his foot and paw," replies Roberts. "He should heal fine, but we'll watch him for several weeks and then remove the cast. We can't let him go to a new home until the cast on his leg is removed and we're sure his paw has healed."

In one corner of the cage, there's a small bowl of dry food next to a bowl of water. On the opposite side of the cage is a tray of cat litter. I haven't seen such a nice bathroom in a long, long time, or for that matter, real fresh food or clean and unfrozen water. Looking at my new living quarters, I think if I didn't feel so bad, I'd feel good—perhaps a strange thing to say, but otherwise true. I am tired, still exhausted from everything I've been through.

Sunlight streams onto the small blanket I rest upon. It's warm and clean, something else I haven't had in a very long time. It even has pictures of kittens and hearts on it. Since I've been homeless, simple things like old rags and sheets in Buster's basement were even appreciated, especially since they were so much better than paper and wet cardboard to sleep upon. How fortunate I am now, especially knowing that I still have a paw, a warm place to recover, and fresh food to eat.

Immediate fears subside as long days follow and I start to feel better. The damage to my paw has been extensive and my recovery from surgery is slow. I guess the healing process always seems that way. Being confined in a cage most of the time, however, make the days seem somewhat boring. I'm used to wandering around from place to place and visiting my friends whenever I want. I'm not used to being confined for any length of time or staying in any one place. Even my confinement in Harvey's storage shed never lasted more than a day or two. Although I miss the camaraderie of my friends, I do like the idea that I don't have to scrounge for food every day. I also don't miss the soggy cardboard boxes that used to drip water onto my head at night while I tried to sleep. I especially don't miss the cold and snow that constantly threatened my survival without a permanent place of shelter. There isn't much I can do here while being pent up in my cage, but although I'm missing a dew claw and toe, my paw feels better with each passing day. That fact alone makes my confinement bearable. I am getting better.

Several weeks have passed now, and I'm able to walk with my cast. Volunteers at the shelter take me to a large room each day so I can wander around and get some exercise. They call it the community room. Walking with a cast on my leg proves difficult to say the least—like a pirate with a peg leg that I saw in an animated movie so long ago. Activity periods in the community room occur several times a day. Even though it's difficult to maneuver with a stiff cast on my leg, I look forward to being out of my cage for a while.

My daily efforts are finally rewarded as my paw heals and the cast is finally removed. My left foot feels so much lighter now without the heavy burden of the cast. My paw looks slightly disfigured than my others, though. But there's still a little fur that covers two of my toes. At least I have most of my toes, as well as full use of my paw. It could have been a lot worse. I've gained a lot more flexibility and am able to jump up onto one of the low windowsills in the community room. I like to sit in front of the large windows and look out at a group of trees that separate a parking lot from the nearby highway.

Normally I'm alone for my daily exercise, but this morning is different. The staff has decided it's time for me to interact with a couple of other cats. To my pleasant surprise, I am introduced to two female cats, both multicolored, one tortoiseshell and one calico. Even with the cast removed, I still have a slight limp as I walk toward them in order to introduce myself. After hanging around Chester and Buster for so long, I'm not very shy about meeting other cats. Besides, it's been awful lonely without my friends around.

"Hi, I'm Patches," I say. Then I remember that the veterinarian hadn't known my original name and I now have another one. "I guess my new name is Figaro."

The other two cats notice my slightly awkward, limited mobility and casually amble over to meet me.

"Hi, my name's Willow," says the tortoiseshell cat. "And her name is Jenna. We had different names as well before we arrived at the shelter. Don't fret about the name change. You'll get used to it."

"I'm really happy to talk with you both. I was getting a little lonely being in a cage or walking about in this room all by myself. Do either of you know how long I've been here? I've lost my entire perception of time."

"Well, we've both been here since the early part of last November," says Jenna. "When both of our owners found out we were going to have kittens, neither one of them wanted us anymore. I guess neither household could afford more mouths to feed. So they brought us here. We both arrived the same week. It happens to a lot of animals. I had three kittens, and Willow had two. We're all alone now. All our kittens have been adopted. We older cats aren't as popular. We sure do miss our kittens. That was several months ago."

"We both had kittens about two months before you came here. Jenna and I were out in this room when we saw two men in oversized winter jackets come running in here with you in an old scraggly blanket with some sort of chain dangling down from your foot. They were in a real hurry, shouting they needed some help. They seemed to be really upset. That was in early January. You've been mending ever since that time, and according to that wall calendar over there with the pictures of spring flowers, it's now the month of March."

"Then you've been here for quite some time now yourselves," I reply to Willow.

"Yes, it's been a while. From what we've noticed, kittens

are usually the first to get new homes. As Jenna mentioned, all of our kittens have been adopted, and I heard one of the volunteers saying that one family is adopting the both of us together next week. Sometimes it's better to adopt two cats at the same time so they keep each other company—as long as they get along with each other. Jenna and I seem to have a lot of things in common, and we get along well together, so we're looking forward to living in the same home. We've finally been spoken for."

"You must be happy to have heard that bit of good news," I reply. "It sure would be nice to have a good home. I had one once. I had two sisters and one brother. They were given away to other families while I was still very young. I don't remember them very well. It's been such a long time now. After my father abandoned us, my mother and I were the only ones left. I was the only one that had the same coloring as my father. I do remember that. Evidently, I got thrown out of my home just a little while before both of you were brought here. You were fortunate not having to deal with living outside in the cold winter weather. I've been living alone on the streets and fending for myself ever since early last fall."

Our conversation continues into the late afternoon and Willow and Jenna tell me about their previous homes and their experiences. They don't remember much about their first homes. They were only a few months old when they left. In turn, I tell them how I had become homeless and how I had met new friends and had survived.

In the days that follow, I tell them about my adventures. I make them smile when I tell them about my experiences with the rats and Harvey Stunk. I tell them about the nights of being entertained at the diner, watching the people eating, and expound about the pranks the rats played on Harvey. I tell them about my silly friend, Bracken, and the incident with Carlo. I tell them about the things I had learned from Chester and Buster, and about the fire that almost cost Buster's life. I tell them how I was able to save him and how my own life was saved, as well as I could remember. And I tell them about my experiences when scrounging for food and searching for shelter. During only a few short months of being a vagabond, I tell them about those experiences, good and bad. And I know those things that I have learned will remain a part of me throughout my life. I am an individual, comprised of events and lives of others. We all are.

Willow and Jenna tell me about their previous homes and how they had lived with other cats. Then they reminisce about what they can remember of their earlier days.

"I don't remember where I was born," says Willow.

"Neither do I," says Jenna.

They don't remember much about their mother, but tell me they do remember that they had brothers who were larger than they were. Each one tells me that they were very young when they were separated from their families. Curiously, though, they seem to share one common memory. They both recall colored hues of purple and blue that danced across the walls in a room where they slept. It makes me wonder about such an odd coincidence. I remember those colors as well.

Several days have passed since I last talked with Willow and Jenna, but I'm here with them again this afternoon in the community room. Tomorrow they'll be leaving for their new home. There are several other cats in here today also. My strength has increased over the many weeks at the shelter, and I have actually gained some weight. I can move around much quicker now without the extra weight of the cast. Jenna and Willow are quick to notice the improved dexterity in my gait as I trot toward them so I can say goodbye.

"My paw looks disfigured," I comment as both Jenna and Willow smile at my approach. I am embarrassed by my appearance.

Willow is quick to respond. "See Terrance over there?"

I look across the room at one of the large holding pens for dogs and see a three-legged Golden Retriever.

"He was taking a walk out in the woods with his owner and wandered off the trail. Some careless hunter had left an old bear trap in the woods from the previous winter, and that poor dog walked right into it. The trap had sharp teeth that tore right into his leg, just like yours except on a much larger scale. His owner got him here to the closest vet before he lost too much blood and saved his life. But Terrance lost his leg. He's only here for another day or two to get checked out, and then he's going home. He's lucky in one way. He has someone who loves him no matter what his condition is.

The owner blames himself for not keeping him on a leash. But he really shouldn't. The hunter is the one to blame. That trap should never have been so close to a residential area. Worse than that, he should not have forgotten about it or even used anything like it at all. Terrance gets around pretty well, though. He makes the best out of a bad situation. What else would you do? Your toes may look a little odd, but at least you have all four feet that you can walk on. You should consider yourself fortunate. It could have been much worse. Don't worry about what it looks like."

I think about Willow's comment and understand what she's trying to tell me—simply be thankful for what I have. "You're absolutely right. I shouldn't be complaining," I reply. "This is actually a happy day for me too. I heard one of the volunteers talking to someone earlier this morning, and it looks like I've also been adopted. I don't even know who the people are or anything about them, but I'm going to have a real home again. Hopefully, this time, it will be a permanent one. I'm not sure when I'm going to be able to leave, though."

"Well, you won't be leaving until they're sure that paw of yours has healed," says Jenna. "I'd guess that'll probably be within a week or so. Congratulations on your adoption. Both of us are leaving tomorrow. So we'll all have new homes. We're going to miss our talks with you, though."

"I'm going to miss both of you too," I say. I know that I won't see them again. Yet, I'm uplifted with the thought that they will soon have a new home. We talk about our individual hopes and fears and then say goodbye to each other at the end of the day. As I watch them leave together, I think about our conversations and the stories we shared. It's strange that they seem so familiar to me. It feels like I'm losing them for a second time. As I sit here in the community room all alone, I think about my past, and wonder when I'll be going to my new home as well.

Chapter 17

Going Home

It's the middle of March. Willow and Jenna have gone, and I am finally cleared for release from the shelter to go to my new home as well. I can walk normally once more, and my quick gait has returned as I've gained more strength. The missing fur on my paw really doesn't bother me now. I am used to how it looks. It's interesting on how your perspective changes relative to appearance and to what really matters.

"You're going to your new home today, big fellow," Dr. Roberts says to me as he picks me up and examines me from nose to tail. "We're really going to miss you. You've been through a lot, and you deserve a good home. Things will be better for you now."

Sam is working, so Abby comes to the shelter by herself with a large cat carrier in hand. She remembers the story Sam had told her, about his trip home with Mittens many years earlier, and decides it might not be safe to have a cat roaming freely in the car while she's driving. The call from the shelter was earlier than expected and surprised them both. It didn't give her or Sam a chance to visit me before my release.

I am in the community room with other cats when she arrives. Kelly points me out to her. Abby appears to be surprised at how large I am. I walk over to her as she enters the room, acknowledging the fact that I'm the cat who's supposed to go home with her. I don't want to miss out on this chance.

"You're one heavy cat," she says as she lifts me into the cat carrier. Her comment reminds me of those very same words I had said to Buster when I had dragged him out of the fire on that cold winter night. Abby shows everyone a picture of her cat Mittens and comments on the uncanny resemblance. She places the cat carrier on the front desk counter while she completes the final paperwork for my adoption. I can see the picture of Mittens and the name printed in bold letters on the border of the photograph. We actually do look alike, except I appear to be twice the size of the cat she once had. I try to get comfortable as she thanks everyone at the shelter for their help, carries me to the car, and places the carrier on the front seat. If I stand up in the carrier, I can barely see over the dashboard.

I've never been inside a cat carrier before, and it's rather cramped for my size. But I don't care. I am about to partake in a new adventure. I'm going to my new home. I twirl round inside the cage several times as I try to maneuver into a more comfortable position. Chester and Buster would be happy for me.

As the car proceeds smoothly down the highway, I think about the only other ride I had ever had in a vehicle. It was the bumpy ride in an old garbage truck with two people who cared enough to save my life. I don't remember much about the rough ride at all, however, even though it seemed as though the truck had bounced and shook as it hit just about every pothole in the road.

I keep peeking up over the top of the car's dashboard to see where I'm going. The buildings and cars whiz by my window. The distractions of all these new images help to lessen my trepidation about going to a place I've never been to before. Sometimes it's difficult to cope with change and the unknown. I've experienced plenty of that. But good changes are always better than bad ones. I have had enough of those.

The travel time from the shelter to my new home seems short, and as Abby drives onto the long dirt driveway that leads to her house, I notice the dense growth of trees and the rock walls that surround the entrance. The driveway runs along the edge of a forest, and the house is the last one in from the main road, somewhat isolated from other houses in the neighborhood. It is two stories high, and its vertical shiplap exterior is colored with a solid brown stain that blends into the surrounding woods. A narrow deck attached to the second floor looks out over a yellow-brown lawn waiting for the first signs of spring. Two French style doors face the driveway, and birdfeeders hang from the bottom of the upper deck directly in front of them. There are all sorts of birds flying from one feeder to another. The hanging bird feeders remind me of the house where I was born, and Chester's house as well. I recognize many kinds of birds because of my mother and Chester showing me, including cardinals, nuthatches, titmouse, and finches. Seeing all those birds make me think about Lilly and the cold nights I had spent watching her looking out at them. My wish for a home and family have finally come true.

I stand up in the carrier, hitting my head against the top. My eyes are wide with excitement and uncertainty. The house looks much larger than my original home. Off to one side of the driveway I can see several large black crows—my favorite birds to watch. They are sitting high up on branches near a back fence that separate the end of the driveway from an abutting forest. They are busy sharing a meal of table scraps left outside for them. There are just so many things to see. It's a lot of information to take in at one time.

"Well, welcome to your new home," Abby says to me as she lifts the carrier from the car into the house. She puts the carrier down in the hallway and opens its door. I very cautiously stick my head out of the small opening and peek around both sides, trying to get acclimated to my new surroundings.

Kali is in the hallway from having slept there all day, and therefore is the first one to greet me. She is so excited that her tail shakes vigorously back and forth. To my surprise, she runs right over to me before I completely exit the carrier.

"Hi, I'm Kali-Cat. Just call me Kali. Welcome to your new home. This will be great. We'll have a new brother." Her tail keeps shaking as she speaks.

Wickett is somewhat more reserved than Kali in accepting me as a new addition to the family and approaches very slowly. I am much larger, and she doesn't know how I'll react. I think it might be better to have her initiate the first action, so I politely sit down in front of Kali and wait for Wickett's approach. As Wickett comes shoulder to shoulder with Kali, I introduce myself to both cats using the second name I have received from the shelter. I think everyone will use the name that appears on my adoption papers, so I decide to stick with that.

As I sit in the hallway, looking around, I say, "This looks like a really big place."

"Don't worry. We'll show you around," Wickett announces very demurely. "Follow us." The three of us slowly make our way to the living room area.

"I'll just let you three get acquainted as best you can," says Abby as we check each other over and leave the hallway. I notice that Abby is watching just to make sure we're getting along.

"Well, at least you don't smell like a wet dog," Wickett states. I give her a quizzical look. "During bad weather," she explains, "we had a few dogs who showed up as strays at the animal shelter. You smell better than they did, but you do smell like the same shelter where we came from a few months ago."

"Did the shelter have a large parking lot with a highway nearby that was separated by a group of trees?" I ask.

"I don't remember," says Wickett, "but I do remember that blankets in the cages had pictures of kittens and hearts."

"That sounds like the same shelter I came from," I reply. "I was homeless and on my own for a long time before I arrived at the animal shelter." While the three of us sit together looking out one of the French doors onto the front lawn, I tell them about my homeless days, the friends I had acquired, my experiences, and how I had ended up at the shelter. I also tell them about meeting Jenna and Willow.

Kali and Wickett don't have a lot to tell me about themselves because they were adopted when they were only about eight weeks old and had been born at the shelter. Being so young, all they can remember is that they each looked like their mothers.

I spend the rest of the day investigating both floors of the house with my new siblings. Their tour includes the upstairs bedrooms, Sam's in-house upstairs office with his computers, Abby's sewing room where one of several, all important cat litter boxes is located, the downstairs master bedroom, and an old cardboard box filled with cat toys. There is even a four-level cat post located in the living room in front of one of the French doors. I can look out onto the front yard from there and see anything that approaches the house from the driveway.

The toy box is perhaps the most awesome thing I have ever seen. I have never seen so many cat toys, or anything that didn't make squeaking sounds unless it was alive. I just sit looking at the old cardboard box with wonder. "What are these strange and wonderful things?" I ask them. So they show me how to play, and the three of us have a very active and informative afternoon. The interaction with my new playmates reminds me of my earlier days as a kitten. It brings back a flood of good memories.

During the next few weeks, Kali and Wickett show me where everything is. It's during that time that my name is changed once again for a third time. This time, it is Abby's and Sam's two boys who come up with my third name. They call me Stimpson. Don't ask me where they got that name. I'll never know—neither does Sam.

Wickett teaches me how to access and use all four levels of the scratch post. I find that scratching on the sisal rope, which is wrapped around the center post, is similar to sharpening my claws on tree trunks, but the rope is much easier on my paws. Kali teaches me how to drink directly from running water under a faucet. For some reason, I find it is actually more refreshing than drinking from a bowl. She reminds me of my friend Chester, who also taught me many useful things. They both take turns showing me views of the forest from the many windows.

I find the third shelf up on the scratch post to actually be my favorite spot for gazing outside. I can watch birds and squirrels from my new perch. Every once in a while, however, I become distracted and think about the outdoors and my old friends.

All three of us get along very well, and we often huddle together in front of the large windows watching the birds outside. It's mid-April when Abby decides it's time to open up the solarium for the first time for everyone to use. The outside temperature is at sixty degrees, but it's seventy-six degrees according to the thermometer hanging inside the solarium—similar to the one at Harvey's diner.

Entering the solarium is like walking into a beautiful summer day even though it is only early spring. All three of us wander cautiously out onto the brick and stone dust floor to examine the new room. The many windowsills offer perfect sitting spots and views of the outside, and the many chairs with pillows offer perfect sleeping accommodations for lazy afternoons. From my viewpoint, it's simply the best room in the house.

Every day the sun shines, Abby opens the inside door from the house to the solarium so the warmth from the room helps to heat the house. The three of us know the instant the door opens because the house's alarm system chimes once. As soon as we hear the chime, we all scamper to the solarium. It's almost like being outdoors—better in some ways because you don't have to worry about the weather, ticks, or fleas.

Abby always knows where we are on sunny afternoons. She finds us sitting on the windowsills intently watching chipmunks and squirrels or sleeping soundly in one of the chairs. I can see myself becoming very spoiled in a short period of time, just like the other two. Of course, being spoiled comes easy in comparison to my earlier winter months.

It's warm in the solarium this morning and Abby picks me up in her arms and says, "This is as close to the outside as we dare let you get. I know you were on your own for a while, but we can't let you wander around outside the house. It might not be safe with all the animals that live in these woods. We don't want you to get hurt or lost. We can open up the outside door to the solarium and close the screen door so you can sniff all those great smells from outside, but that's as close as you can get. So your mouse chasing days are over." Believe it or not, I am okay with that. Besides, I have only chased mice with Chester, and we never really tried to catch any of them.

Just as the sun begins to set and just before the solarium is closed up for the day, we have unexpected company.

Chapter 18

The Visitor

The floor of the solarium is made up of stone dust and bricks spaced in a basket weave pattern. It is constructed that way so you can water hanging plants in the room, and any excess water that spills onto the floor will simply drain into the earth beneath. The only drawback to that convenience, however, means that any ambitious critter like a deer mouse or chipmunk, digging from outside, can eventually dig their way up under the floor and into the solarium through the spaces between the bricks. Leaving the solarium open to the inside of the house means we can come and go as we please, but so can anything else small enough to infiltrate the floor.

Kali spots it first as it runs into the house. The three of us have been in the solarium all afternoon, just waking up from an hour or so of heavy napping. I watch as Wickett chases Kali into the house and think I better join the skirmish as well. I follow them in hot pursuit. We fly down the carpeted hallway like an animated herd of elephants being chased by ninja warriors. Abby is preparing dinner when we skid across the wooden floor in the kitchen. I'm having fun at this point, not really knowing what I'm chasing. But we all lose our traction, and Kali slams head-first into one of the kitchen chairs, totally out of control due to speed, lack of friction, and momentum from a little too much weight.

"What are you guys doing?" Abby asks loudly.

We all stop short, surprised by her sudden question to our unexpected assault on her kitchen. That's when both Abby and I see the tiny deer mouse running for his life.

Like skilled hunters, we surround the poor little guy. Abby stands speechless, stunned. To her surprise, as well as mine, Kali and Wickett turn and nonchalantly walk out of the kitchen. I'm astounded by their retreat. I'm not sure what I should do next. Evidently the other two have decided it's too much like work to continue the chase. They've completely lost interest, leaving Abby to take care of the new toy they've discovered.

"Are you two giving up?" I ask Kali and Wickett as they leave the room.

"Yeah, we're tired," Wickett replies. "You catch him."

"Thanks a lot, you two," Abby says as she watches them walk away. "You're no help whatsoever! You chase a mouse into the house and then just give up. I don't suppose you're going to be much help either." Abby looks at me and reaches for a dishtowel so she can trap the mouse herself. But as she tries to throw the dishtowel over him, he scatters out into the living room, prompting me to chase him once again.

I bound into the living room and chase the mouse until he scurries under a large bookcase. I'm too big to fit under the lower shelf. Sam is reading a book and stands upon hearing the commotion and watching my unsuccessful pursuit.

"Did you see where the mouse went?" Abby asks Sam as she runs into the living room, dishtowel in hand.

"Yep, he ran right under the bookcase," replies Sam, slightly surprised by the sudden activity.

"What are you going to do?" Abby says to me as I try to peek under the small opening at the base of the bookcase, waiting for the mouse's next action. "I guess I was wrong. Apparently, your mouse chasing days aren't over."

I smile at her remark.

"Stimpson's just lying in front of the bookcase, waiting," Sam comments. "Smart cat."

"Well, at first, I was happy about the other two trying to catch the mouse," replies Abby, "but apparently they got tired of the whole thing and left the chase completely up to Stimpson and me."

Sam eyes the five shelves full of books. "We could take all those books off the shelves and move the bookcase so that we can chase the mouse back out. Then we can have another chance of catching him. But waiting for him to come out is probably the easiest and smartest approach. Let's wait and see what Stimpson is going to do."

I wait patiently in front of the bookcase while the mouse hides underneath. Sam turns on the television to watch the five o'clock news, watching me also. Patience can sometimes be a virtue—something everyone should consider before making rash decisions. Both Chester and Buster taught me that. They taught me to think things through before making abrupt decisions. They made me somewhat street smart.

The one-hour news cast ends just as the mouse emerges from underneath the heavy bookcase. My patience finally pays off, and I quickly place my right paw directly on top of the little guy. I immediately grab him lightly by the scruff of his neck with my teeth so he can't get away—but gently, as if he were a kitten.

"Gotcha!" I exclaim.

Sam watches the entire time. I look up at Abby, mouse in mouth, wondering what to do with him. She has a surprised expression on her face. I think she's proud of me for being their street smart cat. I hold the mouse just tightly enough so Abby can gather him up with the dishtowel. She quickly opens the front door and lays the dishtowel on the ground, releasing him to the outside.

I think about Amos, Ollie, and Olive as I watch Abby free the mouse. I'll never forget the kind act they had once done for me on a cold January day. They had saved my life. I've simply taken the opportunity to return an act of kindness once given to me. That's the least I can do.

Most days slip by quietly. There are exceptions, though. One night in the second week of May, bloodcurdling screams emerge from the forest.

Chapter 19

The Crow

Loud, nightmarish cries wake Sam out of a sound sleep. He barely sees the digital numbers on the alarm clock. His eyes are still blurry from sleep. He had gone to bed an hour earlier, and it's just after midnight. The screaming cries of terror bring him sitting straight up out of bed.

"What in the world are those cries?" Sam asks Abby, who also wakes up. He quickly jumps out of bed and opens the shade to the bedroom window. It's pitch black outside. "No moon tonight. I can't see a thing. It sounds like someone's in horrible pain."

Sam goes to another room, retrieves a flashlight, and returns to the bedroom. He opens up the window and shines the light through the screen into the forest. "I still can't see anything. I'd better go outside and see what's going on."

"Get something on your feet," declares Abby. "There are rocks, tree branches, and building materials on that side of the house that we haven't cleaned up yet. It'll be hard walking out there in your bare feet and you certainly don't want to step on any old rusty nails."

"Okay," says Sam as he puts on a pair of hard-soled slippers and ambles down the hallway toward the front door. "I wish we had some lights on that side of the house. One of these days I'll take the time to install a few. I always seem to put things off until they have to be done. Additional lights are just another project that hasn't been done yet," he mumbles aloud as he reaches the front door.

"I think it's called procrastination," Abby replies, giving Sam an understanding look as she follows behind him and stops at the door.

Sam begrudgingly shakes his head in agreement and steps out onto the front deck that extends down the length of the house toward the edge of the forest. The night air is cool and as he hurries toward the end of the deck, the screeching sounds become louder. He walks down the stairs and onto the sloping ground that extends from the house into the forest. As he approaches the edge of the woods, the cries seem louder but intermittent as he gets closer to its source. His flashlight searches the woods and its beam shines over the stacked tree limbs that still wait to be cut for firewood. The piles of wood remind Sam of more work he has to do. Old lumber is piled up from decking restorations and new construction that is still ongoing.

As the beam from his flashlight focuses on something large and black, the ear-piercing cries stop and then start once again. Sitting on top of a pressure treated two-by-four stud in the pile of lumber is a large black crow. He is standing on one leg and screeching as if he is crying for help. Two piercing eyes reflect light from Sam's flashlight and appear to glow in the dark directly behind the crow. The glaring eyes belong to the neighbor's cat, George, who is ready to pounce upon the defenseless bird. Sam picks up a rock and tosses it toward the cat in order to scare him away. There are plenty of stones around, and it takes three throws before George finally gives up, believing he might get hit. The crow remains motionless, unmoving during the entire episode.

"Are you hurt?" Sam asks as if he expects an answer.

The crow stands on one leg, watching Sam. Thinking the cat has retreated and might no longer be a threat to his survival, his cries for help subside.

"Are you hurt?" Sam asks again in a low tone of voice as he slowly approaches the crow. Making no attempt to flee, the crow remains motionless. Sam places the flashlight under his arm and gently picks the crow up with both hands. He makes no attempt to evade capture, nor does he try to peck Sam with his long, sharp beak. He just waits to be scooped up and saved.

Sam hurries back to the house holding the crow at arm's

length with the flashlight wedged underneath his arm. Trying to carry both the crow and the flashlight at the same time is a bit cumbersome. Abby is at the front door as Sam approaches the house. Sam hollers, "Abby, see if you can find that old bird cage we stored in the basement last year. Looks like this crow has an injured wing of sorts. If we don't bring him in tonight, something will eventually attack him, especially if he can't fly. He just let me pick him up, so something's not right."

"I know exactly where that old cage is," replies Abby. She disappears from the front door entrance while Sam waits on the outside deck by the door, holding onto the crow. Sam doesn't dare enter the house without somehow confining the crow because he's worried that the crow might get loose from his grip. If that happens, they'll have the possibility of a crow hobbling about the house or, worse yet, trying to fly from room to room. Within minutes, Abby returns without the cage.

"That's an awful small cage for such a large bird," Abby exclaims. "So I brought up the old playpen we had for the kids when they were little and opened it up in the sewing room. It has mesh sides, and we can tie a quilt over the top so he can't get out into the house. That way he'll have a little room so he can walk around a bit."

"Sounds like a great idea," says Sam as he enters the house holding the crow with both hands. "He is kind of big."

The crow is passive and makes no attempt to fight or escape as Sam places him in the playpen.

"I'll put water and sunflower seeds in some containers for him," says Abby.

The crow just sits there and watches as Abby places the food and water into the playpen then ties a quilt over the top.

"That's all we can do for him tonight," says Sam. "At least he'll be safe. I'm sure he knows we're trying to help him. Otherwise, he would have been fighting me to get free. They're really smart birds."

"So, was it the crow that was making all those horrible sounds we were hearing?" asks Abby. "Since there are no more piercing cries from the forest, I assume that's what it was."

"Yeah," says Sam. "The next door neighbor's cat was about to pounce on the poor bird. That's probably why he was crying for help. If he looks worse in the morning or doesn't get better in a couple of days, we should take him up to the wildlife sanctuary just north of here and have him checked out."

The sewing room is adjacent to the hallway that leads to the front door and the downstairs bedroom. Before they go back to bed, they check the playpen once more to make sure the sides and top are intact. The crow just sits, watching.

I had been sleeping on the cat post in the living room and woke up when the hall lights were turned on. I heard Abby talking about a birdcage as she went down to the cellar.

I can hear Sam and Abby's conversation as they return to their bedroom at the end of the hallway. I hadn't gotten involved earlier because I figured they didn't need additional help during all the commotion. But things have calmed down a bit and my curiosity is getting the better of me. It's time that I check things out for my own. I haven't seen a real crow up close before. I quietly walk into the sewing room and am surprised to see a playpen instead of a birdcage. The crow watches me as I enter the room.

The crow speaks first, knowing he's somewhat safe within the confines of the playpen. "Hello there, Mr. Cat. I just barely got away a few minutes ago from one of your friends next door. I thought I was a goner out there in the woods all by myself."

"First of all, I'm not Mr. Cat," I reply. "My name is Stimpson. And secondly, if you're talking about the next door neighbor's cat, he's not a friend of mine. I don't even like him. He's really obnoxious. He hangs around our house a lot and chases the birds away that I like to watch. You don't need to worry about me, though. I'm not here to try and harm you in any way. I've just never had an opportunity to talk with a crow. I don't get to go outside much anymore. But I do like to watch you crows flying in and out of the forest. It's amazing how you navigate between trees and branches. I used to watch crows when I was a kitten and lived in another place. I liked to watch them chase away the hawks from getting the little birds around my house."

"Well, thanks for the compliment. My name is Inky. Kinda fits, don't you think?"

"Very fitting. I agree. So what happened to you tonight?"

"Well, I was getting ready to fly back up to my nest, which is about thirty feet off the ground in one of those oak trees next to your house. I had just finished eating some food that I found on the ground when a yellow tiger cat, your next door neighbor, snuck up behind me and swatted the side of my wing. I managed to evade another quick attack by hopping up on some lumber."

"How's the wing now?" I ask.

"Well, I can't lift it very high right now. It aches."

"So what happened after you managed to escape from the cat's attack the first time?"

"I started hollering for my parents to help because I figured that cat would try to finish me off. I think his name is George. I've heard people calling for him sometimes when he doesn't go home for the night. I wish they wouldn't leave him out all the time. Before my parents heard my cries, the people who live here got to me first and saved me. They've always been nice to us. They throw out a lot of food scraps for us as well as sunflower seeds, especially during the winter months when food is so scarce. They also put out suet for the woodpeckers, and we kinda eat some of that too at times."

"Yeah, that's Sam and Abby. They adopted me from an animal shelter a few months ago. I saw several of you by the back fence when I first arrived here. This is my new home. If you like, I'll tell you how I got to live here later. I should let you get some rest now. It's getting late. I hope you feel better. I'll talk with you again tomorrow."

"Thanks. I'll look forward to it. I never expected I would share experiences and have an affable discussion with a cat."

I laugh at his remark, and as I leave the sewing room, I think about how smart that crow must really be. He used a word like affable. I'm not even sure what the word means.

Early the next morning, Inky wakes and finds me sitting next to the playpen. I'm anxious to continue our conversation.

"Well, good morning," says Inky, a little surprised by my early morning company.

"I didn't mean to wake you. I just thought I'd sit here quietly until you woke up on your own. How are you feeling?" I ask.

"I feel better, but my wing aches, and I still can't raise it very high. It will probably be a couple of days until I get the full use of it back again and I'm able to fly. I'm glad they didn't try to put me into a birdcage. I saw the one they have. It's over there in the corner of the room. It's made for the size of a finch. It would have been really restricting for my size, a real head bumper—like putting an eagle into a hamster cage. There's a lot more room in this playpen. I can move around better in here."

"Yeah, that playpen is about the size of the cage I was in at the shelter when my foot was in a cast."

My reply starts a conversation that continues on and off for several days. I tell Inky about everything that had happened to me. It has only been about eight months since I first became homeless, but in people years, that's equal to about five years. Time is just a matter of relevance. I talk about the friends I have made and the things I have learned. Inky, in turn, tells me that he was born just that spring and that he has just recently started flying. He tells me his parents are teaching him who his predators are and how to tell whether a person is to be feared just by recognizing their characteristics and how they act toward animals.

"We like to mob and drive away owls and hawks. I've been practicing navigating through the trees. It's really fun—well, unless you hit a tree branch when you aren't paying attention to where you're going. That can be really embarrassing, and it can bruise more than one's ego. We dive through treetops and chase the hawks until they're a goodly distance away from our homes. We can make their lives unbearable at times. It kind of reminds me of the stories you've told me about Harvey Stunk and your friends playing pranks on him. We know the hawks have to find food just like we do, but my parents would prefer it if they didn't try to add us and some of our smaller friends who live in our area to their menu."

Inky and I share interesting stories with one another. Several days pass while his wing continues to heal. I introduce Kali and Wickett to Inky, and he understands that not all cats are interested in trying to harm a large bird like himself, especially when two of the aforementioned cats can't even finish catching a mouse because it's too much like work.

Three days after saving Inky from George, Abby decides to take Inky outside with her to see if he is ready to leave his cage and fly home. Abby does a small wash load every day and hangs the clothes outside to dry on sunny days.

Sam has strung up a makeshift clothesline between some trees at the edge of the forest. A real clothesline with pulleys is on his list of home improvement projects to be done, but like his list of other projects, he hasn't gotten to that one either.

Abby places Inky on her shoulder while she carries the laundry basket. He continues to sit passively while she takes clothespins out of a basket and snaps them over the line to hang each piece of laundry to dry. Inky never makes any attempt to leave. He stays on her shoulder and returns to the house where he knows there's plenty of food and water in the playpen. Crows are pretty smart birds. Inky knows that he has a good thing going for himself while he is healing.

Two days later, however, when Abby is at the clothesline with Inky on her shoulder, I watch through the screen door of the solarium and see him gently spread his wings and lift himself effortlessly into the air. It's time to go home. He circles over her three times and then just as abruptly as he had come into our lives, he leaves. "I'm going to miss your company," Abby shouts to him as she watches Inky settling onto a high branch looking down at her. He caws to her, saying goodbye, looks in my direction, and then flies off over the tree tops and disappears.

I've lost another friend. I sadly understand that. But the more I think about it, the more I realize that even though friends leave, you don't really lose them, they are always there, within you. Even though you may not see them as often, you always have the memories of your experiences with them. That's something you can always cherish.

The very next day, as I watch Abby hanging the laundry out to dry, I hear two crows cawing loudly on a branch high above her. She looks up as one crow looks down at her and caws.

"I know you don't understand what I'm saying," says Inky, "but I wanted to thank you once again for saving my life." He briefly faces the larger crow, caws, turns back around, looks downward at Abby once again, and says, "This is my dad." The larger crow caws, as if to also thank her, and both of them spread their wings, lift high into the air, circle, and disappear above the treetops. Abby may not have understood the conversation, but I'm sure she knows it was Inky and one of his parents returning for a final goodbye. I doubt she'll ever forget the moment.

I miss my conversations with Inky, and I spend many of my afternoons in the solarium watching the skies for him. I wonder if I'll ever see him again. You just never know how one life can affect another.

Daily, I watch Abby as she takes the laundry out to the clothesline. But once in a while, I see her step onto a dark pathway that enters the forest, a natural archway of trees and branches, and she disappears for several hours at a time. I wonder where she goes.

Chapter 20

A Walk in the Woods

It's mid-afternoon. I hear Abby and Sam talking about going out to shop for a few things and then to a restaurant for an early dinner. Sam steps outside to shut off the pump in the pond that powers the waterfall. He figures they might return late, and he doesn't want the pump to run all night. He shoos all of us cats into the house so we won't take the opportunity to sneak outside while he has the screen door open. I return to the solarium just before he's had the chance to shut the connecting door to the house. Sam still thinks I'm in the house with the other two cats. I head over to the windowsill in the back corner of the solarium and sit there looking out over the front lawn. Sam has carelessly left the outside screen door to the solarium slightly open, and he doesn't see me.

The neighbor's yellow tiger cat, the one that had attacked Inky, is sprawled out on the lawn directly in front of one of the solarium windows. It looks to me like he has trapped something. I'm not very happy about having this intruder on my lawn. I consider this to be my territory, just like Buster had his. In addition, I don't like George chasing the smaller animals that I like to watch.

I see Sam outside by the pond. He's busy. The partially open screen door is really tempting. Since the opportunity has presented itself, I'll take it. I don't need to hesitate any longer. It's time to chase the intruder from my front lawn. I bound outside through the small opening at the screen door, and with one short jump from the deck to the ground, I land onto a grassy embankment that leads to the pond and the front lawn. I quickly round the corner of the solarium and see that George has trapped a tiny brown deer mouse. I can see his tail quiver from underneath an overlapping paw.

"What do you think you're doing?" I demand. I'm a bit irritated that George continues to be the obnoxious and self-serving cat that he is.

"I'm gonna eat this tasty-looking little morsel," George replies. He mockingly stares directly at me while he speaks.

"No you're not."

"Oh yes I am," says George and, without any provocation, he immediately jumps at me with his front claws stretched out as he pounces and leaves the stunned mouse behind. George and I are about the same size, but I have one major advantage. I've been taught to wrestle by one of the best trainers—Buster. And with the precise execution of a well-rehearsed hammerlock hold, one that Buster surely would have been proud of, I wrestle George to the ground so he can't move. No matter how hard he struggles, George can't free himself. He finally realizes that it's senseless to continue the fight.

"I give up. You win," says George in angered frustration.

"Are you going to leave?" I ask.

"Yeah, sure, you can have the stupid mouse," George replies. And with that agreeable response, I release George, who then runs as fast as he can toward his own house without looking back.

I turn to see if the mouse has survived our tussle and find him to be unscathed as well as relieved that I've chased George away. He's surprised when I provide added reassurance of his wellbeing and say, "Don't worry, I'm not going to eat you."

"That's a relief," says the mouse. "This is the second time you've been nice to me."

"What do you mean?"

"Well, a few weeks ago, I dug my way up under the floor in your house and three of you cats chased me all over the place. Fortunately, you were the only one who remained interested in catching me. I say fortunately because you didn't hurt me, and I got safely removed to the outdoors. I want to thank you for that thoughtful act of kindness. My name is Toby."

"I remember you. Our foot brakes didn't work so well that afternoon as we chased you into the house and skidded across the kitchen floor. It was fun for us, except maybe for Kali, who crashed headlong into a chair. It didn't hurt her, though; she's got a hard head. But I guess it wasn't so much fun for you. I'm just glad I could help you again today. You deer mice all look alike, being brown and small and all, so I didn't recognize you. My name is Stimpson."

"Well, I'm very happy to meet you. I do look a little different from other deer mice, though," replies Toby. "My tail is a little shorter than most, and the very tip of my left ear is chewed off, thanks to George. He almost managed to catch me a while ago. It was a close call."

"Well, you'd better get home before George decides to return where he's not wanted. I should get back inside my own house as well."

"Thanks again. I won't forget your kindness, even if you are a cat," says Toby jokingly. He sits directly in front of me, whiskers twitching as he talks.

I smile at his remark, and step back up onto the deck in order to enter the solarium. The door is closed. I can't get back into the house.

"Ah-oh," I mutter out loud to Toby. "I think I'm shut out. I never thought to look back and see if Sam had noticed I got out. I was in too big a rush to chase George out of here." I look around and realize Toby has already gone and that I've been talking to myself.

I realize that I have been in too much of a rush to tackle George, and I remember that Chester had warned me to be careful about wandering outside and straying too far. That's how he got separated from his first family. But Chester's new family always remembers when they let him outside. My new family doesn't even know I'm stuck outside the house.

Now what am I going to do? I ask myself.

An hour later, Abby asks Sam, "Have you seen Stimpson?"

"No. I haven't seen him since you fed all three of them an early supper," Sam replies. "I closed the solarium up and shut the waterfall off early because we're going out shopping this afternoon and then out to eat. He was in the solarium with the other two cats at the time, but I shooed them all into the house. Then I went outside and shut off the pump to the waterfall. I checked to make sure no one was left behind and didn't see any of them. He's got to be inside the house somewhere."

"He's probably sleeping in a new spot," Abby replies. "He's pretty resourceful at finding different places to nap. Besides, he's still exploring parts of the house. Let's go out and get some of these errands done."

Not knowing whether or not Sam and Abby are looking for me, I figure it might be a smart idea to find some sort of temporary shelter just in case I can't get back inside the house before they leave. That type of strategy has become part of my survival instincts—plan ahead and prepare for the unknown. It's only mid-afternoon, but there's a noticeable chill in the air. After all, it's still only late May.

Maple and oak trees surround the property. Those types of trees are familiar to me because they are the same kind of trees that grew in my old neighborhood. At the edge of the lawn, there's a much denser growth of a variety of trees and vegetation. I don't recognize some of them. It's like living in a totally different world in this new place. There aren't any tenement buildings here. There are fewer houses, more woods, and, of course, Sam's man-made pond with the small waterfall that runs during the day.

I can either stay next to the house or do a little exploring. And, of course, there's my sense of curiosity, which always gets the best of me. I feel a simultaneous mixture of anticipation and excitement. It's time to explore a little. I step off the deck and cautiously walk across the arched bridge that leads to the forest. Reaching the end, I step down onto the top of a grassy slope and approach the edge of the forest. Ahead of me lays a dense undergrowth of saplings and an opening that leads to a well-defined pathway.

A small stone marker announces the entrance to the wooded trail, reminding me of another path I once walked. Only this time I'm alone, and there is no arbor to welcome my entrance. There are just so many new things to see, and the smells of the forest are overwhelming to my senses. The forest convinces me to continue. Besides, it's the same pathway I've seen Abby enter on several occasions. It must lead somewhere.

The dry leaves remaining on the floor of the forest from the previous fall crackle under my weight as I step onto the trail. The smells of the fresh earth are released with my every step. Gray squirrels scurry up and down the trees as I start to follow the old wood's path. The old trail is well worn from many years of continued use, and even though there is heavy, dense undergrowth, the trail is noticeably perceptible to the eye.

I enter the woods and notice the pile of lumber that Inky had told me about. The stack of wood still remains off to the side of the path. Sam obviously hasn't done anything about cleaning it up yet. I walk past the pile and think about Inky's encounter with the neighbor's cat. I wonder where Inky lives in this forest.

Before continuing along the path, I glance over my shoulder and look back at the house to get my bearings and a sense of direction. I walk along the trail and come to a rivulet on my left that leads to a larger pool of water. The sound of running water entices me to leave the trail and walk down a short embankment. I stop at the water's edge to look at the combined beauty of water and forest. I sip the refreshing flow of water. It's cold and clear and trickles across my toes.

Pausing in front of the large wetland, I realize that I'm not doing what I had previously advised my friend Bracken to do. I remember saying to him, "Pay attention to where you're going." With that thought in mind, I quickly look back over my shoulder once again and can barely see the second story of my new home. I pivot, retrace my steps, and climb back up the hill until I return to the old trail. It's not time to turn back, though. I'm just too curious to find out where the old pathway leads. Perhaps it will provide some answers to my past.

The old pathway lures me onward.

Unheeded by my own advice to others, I continue east along the trail. I know the direction because the sun is seeking a later afternoon sky toward the west. The sun is almost at my back now, and the moss that grows on the sides of a few trees confirm my north and south directions. My father had taught me well during our only walk in the woods.

Across from me, on the opposite side of the pooled water, there are two huge brown dogs, larger than any dog I have ever seen before, even larger than Carlo. One of them has some sort of crooked twigs on its head. Those must hurt. Whatever the animals are, they are getting a drink of water. I have never seen anything like them before. They're watching me. The sounds from my own footsteps echo loudly as the leaves crunch underneath my feet. The crackling sound alarms them. They raise their heads abruptly, turn away, and with white tails pointed straight into the air, sprint in the opposite direction. Within seconds, they are no longer visible.

I continue to follow the path as it narrows into a twilight of thick, low overhanging branches. I travel quite a distance before I turn once again to look over my shoulder. Now I can no longer see my house. Although it's getting later in the afternoon, there's still plenty of daylight, however, and despite the fact that I should stay closer to home, I hike further into the forest. The path has to lead somewhere. Perhaps my new adventure will provide me with a better understanding of nature and myself. Perhaps it will lead to a better understanding of the conversations I had with my father on one afternoon so long ago. Perhaps there is a reason for this old trail and why I'm here—now.

The pathway rambles. Time to consider my direction of travel. I have been going directly east. So, in order to return home, all I have to do is to reverse my direction and travel west. It should be relatively easy to return home. So I continue.

Within moments of making my decision, I hear the shrill cries of a hawk high above my head. There's a sudden swoosh as feathers from enormous wings touch the tips of my ears. Outstretched talons startle me as they barely miss me. Apparently, a red-tailed hawk is considering me as a possible large dinner for his evening meal. His mixed brown and white markings, enormous wing span, and size make him a very distinguishable predator, just as Inky had described his encounters with them during one of our many conversations.

"I really don't want to be your next meal," I shout loudly toward the clouds. Perhaps he can hear me, but it probably won't make a difference no matter what I say. I wonder what his next direction of attack will be. I only hope the hawk might change his mind—a foolish gesture on my part.

I watch as the hawk circles for another attack and drops down from the sky once again. I'm within the confines of the forest, but I'm still on the open pathway. I hear the raspy high-pitched screeching sound as he approaches with his talons stretched outward once again.

I crouch down, waiting for the inevitable, ready to protect myself as best I can. He's fast and deadly in his approach. Just before the hawk reaches me, a small brown mouse darts out from behind an old tree stump, totally distracting the hawk and the focus of his flight path. Confused as to which prey he's after and too slow to make a choice, both the mouse and I elude the hawk as he narrowly misses a low hanging tree branch. The hawk flies back up high into the sky in order to resolve a new plan of attack, circles, and starts down once again focused on one large meal—a cat—me.

I watch as a cluster of seven very large black crows interrupt the red-tailed hawk's flight path as he reaches the top of the trees on a downward spiral. They are faster, more maneuverable, and intercept the hawk's flight, causing total chaos to his intent. I'm relieved at the turn of events as they chase his tail feathers and caw at him unmercifully, forcing him to fly back up over the treetops. The hawk changes his direction and soars upward into the clear sky away from the trees, avoiding his unwanted company. There are too many crows for him to argue with, and they outmaneuver him with speed and dexterity. He quietly leaves the area, perhaps to search for a meal elsewhere. At least it's not me.

I'm not going to be someone else's food for the day. The mouse darts back out onto the path and watches the crows chase the unwanted hawk. It's hard not to notice that he has a short tail and a half-bitten ear. I look down at the small deer mouse and say, "Thanks Toby. You just saved me from that hawk."

"What goes around comes around. As small as I am, I'm glad I could do something. Looks like your buddy, Inky, finished the job. Hawks are as dangerous to me as most cats are. When I step out from a hole into open blades of grass, I never know what shadow might come cruising from above. Those crows really got the best of that hawk this time, though," Toby chuckles.

"I thought one of those crows looked a little smaller than the others in that group. You're probably right; one of those crows must have been Inky. It's so great to have friends that help one another, isn't it?" Before Toby could reply I ask, "What are you doing here anyway?"

"After you saved me from George, I noticed you couldn't get back into your house. I was curious as to where you were going, so I followed you."

"Well, you should return home now before it gets dark. I'm going to follow it for a while longer. There's something about this old trail that compels me to continue my journey further into the woods. I need to find out where it leads."

Chapter 21

Continuum

The path narrows and the further I progress, the less defining it becomes. There is an old stone wall to my right that follows me. It tells me its age with signs of displaced rocks from its top and open gaps in its walls that stagger its length. Broken tree limbs are prevalent and hamper my steps along the path, and I have to either jump over or walk around them at times. As I continue along the pathway, I look over my shoulder and notice the sun is to my back and is lower in the sky, touching the tops of the trees. I know that if I don't arrive at my final destination soon, dusk surely will.

I cross under a natural archway formed by two trees that have fallen toward each other from opposite sides of the path. They have collapsed onto one another, each one holding the other upright, probably by the wind from an earlier storm. Each tree has stopped the other from reaching the ground. I cross under them and see a white glow in the distance.

The deeper into the forest I go, the thicker the leaves become, causing the light in the distance to fade in and out as an infrequent breeze moves the branches from side to side. My footsteps sink deeper as I creep my way forward onto the on-going path less used. Large animal tracks have sunken into the thick blanket of leaves where I walk, and my paws fit within the depths of their imprint. I hear the snap of branches and the rustle of leaves to my left and see a group of the same large brown animals I had seen earlier. There are four of them this time, and as I edge my way off the path to get a better view, they hear my footsteps and pick up their heads. Alarmed at my presence, they quickly turn and dart further into the woods, their tails waving a white goodbye as they disappear into the underbrush. They are strange-looking dogs, but how majestically they glide through the thicket.

I return to the path, and the terrain becomes hilly. I continue down a steep ravine and climb back up to the opposite ridge where the thick overhead branches open up into a small clearing. I pass through nature's doorway, and the white glow I had seen earlier shines brighter than ever as it emanates from sunlight reflected from a field of granite stones that lay before me in serried rows. The sight is completely mesmerizing. The old stone wall that has followed me wraps itself around the stone tablets as if holding back the encroaching forest, trying to protect their timeless existence. I step into the openness. I've seen a similar sight once before—in an afternoon that seemed so long ago—with my father. I'm in a graveyard once again.

A large stone monument several feet in height greets my entrance, but instead of names and dates on the finished surface, there is nothing but weathered stone. Time has washed names and dates away. Nothing remains but the invincible stone itself, leaving no trail of remembrance, only an empty symbol of a memory that was once there.

This cemetery is smaller and covets fewer tablets than the other one I had visited once before. But these tablets are different from others I have seen previously. In addition to names and dates, many of them have pictures of cats and dogs chiseled into their hard granite surfaces.

A faint breeze wafts across my face as I wander among the stones. The deafening solitude is distracted only by the sound of a nearby car. The well-mowed grass extends outward to a front gate, a long distance from me, and it meets the road. I see two people who have stopped to visit one of the stones near the front entrance—a tribute of remembrance. Leaves dance at the back of the cemetery near the forest's edge and sunlight scatters across the face of the tablets. One stone in particular coruscates and draws my gaze to weatherworn letters I have seen once before, on the border of an old photograph—"MITTENS". I realize the old trail has led me to a pet cemetery, one that Abby often visits.

Time lingers as the sun drops slowly below the treetops. Overhanging tree limbs filter the sunlight from an evening sky that touches the horizon and begins to darken as the light slowly disappears. The trail is no longer well defined. Darkness is eminent. It's time to return home.

Knowingly, the trail has accomplished its purpose. It has led me to where I am supposed to be—a time of self-reflection. I listen to the silence. I've stayed too long and will never be able to follow the trail at night. The darkness will swallow the path before I can return. It might be a smart idea to find a safe place for the night. A pine tree just off the pathway at the edge of the cemetery looks like a good spot. There's a soft layer of pine needles at its base, sheltered by ferns and low branches, and offers a suitable refuge. I curl up under the base of the tree, wrap my tail around myself as I've done on so many other occasions in my past, and settle down for the night. I've slept outside many nights before like this, but never in a forest. Sleeping in a forest should be "a piece of cake" compared to finding shelter for the night from a winter snowstorm. That expression brought back memories of my father and I, when we had listened to the three J's talking about a shorter version of their Tai Chi form—a cherished remembrance of our walk together that dwells within me. I remember the conversation I had with my father while we wandered among the old stone tablets in that unattended graveyard, hidden from the world in a time-forgotten orchard. I think about Abby's hikes through the forest to this site and understand why she made those trips. I think about what my father had tried to explain to me when we stood together in a lonely, empty place. His message is so crystal clear to me. It all makes sense to me now. It didn't then. After all this time, I finally understand what he was trying to tell me.

There are always those moments that remain with us no matter what our age is. I can still picture my father and me sitting next to that weathered gravestone, split and partially enveloped by a once younger oak tree that had itself aged over time and yet still lived. I think my father was trying to tell me that as that oak tree grew from an acorn, its age was defined by rings of time within its core. Those rings stayed with it forever throughout its life, not unlike the years of our lives as they are sometimes etched into stone. As one life begins, another one comes to an end. Nature envelops the past, and life begins once again.

We are part of a continuum, reminding us that we exist as one with nature, both in life and in death. Each life affects another, no matter the form of life. There is an interaction that binds us together. We are all unique, and we will always continue to be. That's the way of our universe, a pattern we do not truly understand and perhaps never will. My father had tried to tell me he'd always be there for me. But when he never returned home, I thought he had just left. I had been bitter and resentful about his sudden departure without his goodbye. It was so crystal clear to me now what he had tried to tell me all along. He was dying.

Those moments he paused while we had walked together were for the both of us. He had gone out that cold January day knowing he'd never return. He didn't want us to worry about him. He knew I would eventually come to understand where he had gone. He had returned to a place where he knew there would be no weathered stone for him, but he knew that once I understood, I would never forget. There would be no marker, no tablet to visit. But his presence was deep within me. I would always love him and miss him and not forget. He had returned there to die—a place we had shared together.

I miss him and that will never change. I guess I also understand something else that I have never considered before—not to judge someone's actions too quickly, for they may not be what you think they are. My bitterness is gone; only sorrow and regret remain—regret that I hadn't had more time to spend with him.

I have all these thoughts, and it's pitch black now. The sounds of the forest are like no others I have ever heard before. Some animals are beginning to wake, and others are retiring for the night. A cool breeze continues to touch the tree limbs hanging above me and cause the audible silence of the forest to be a low, steady ring, wanting to be heard. The odor of pine and bark from a dry forest follows as if chased by the breeze, and I lay here under the tree breathing in the refreshing earthy smells of nature. I am part of everything around me. My old family is here within me and my new family is waiting for me.

Clouds part, revealing stars that pepper the night sinking the darkness as the scattered light touches the treetops. There is no moon, only the bright stars from a swollen night. I have never seen anything like it before. Starlight falls onto the old trail like strands of golden hair, and the revelation of my father's message sweeps through me like a cool breeze caressing my very soul. I'll return to my new home in the morning. The fragrant smell of the pine needles is calming and the quiet whispers of the forest lull me to sleep.

Chapter 22

Return

"To wish that certain things didn't happen is to wish that I am not myself."
—Dr. Mary Pipher, "The Shelter of Each Other"

A dawn-soaked morning greets me. It's the itching that causes me to awaken earlier than I usually do. It's the unpleasant irritation of pesky fleas. They are an unwanted insect alarm clock. I haven't had fleas since I was homeless. I have almost forgotten what they were like. Except for my scratching, the forest remains quiet, and the air is still. The stars become scarce as the morning sun changes the black sky to an odd greenish color and then to gold as the sunlight creeps over the trees. I sit up, stretch, look back with a fondness toward the cemetery, and take my first step, knowing I can start over and reverse my direction toward home. By the time I retrace my steps and return to the house, I figure everyone will be looking for me.

Once Sam and Abby realize I'm not around for breakfast, they'll quickly come to the conclusion I'm not in the house. I'm always there for food.

Like an old friend, the trail leads me homeward. It has provided the answers that I've sought for such a long time now and has demanded nothing in return, except for perhaps a request to better understand the living things that surround me. The forest is quiet and nothing stirs. It's as if it is watching me, wanting to ensure my safe return. The sky is quiet and there are no hawks—all is clear and uneventful.

By mid-morning, I see the rooftop of my home among the trees. I follow the path and pass the small stone marker that announces the entrance to the wood's trail. A slight breeze tickles the tops of the trees and they wiggle next to each other as if to wave goodbye. I hear my name being called as I leave the edge of the forest, run up the grassy slope, across the bridge, and toward the house. Sam and Abby see me trotting toward them, and they excitedly call my name. Without hesitation, I run and jump right up into Abby's outstretched arms. I can tell she'll always remember me.

They both seem a little rattled by my disappearance. "Don't you ever scare us like that again. We'll have to be more careful about using the outside screen door from the solarium. I think we know what happened and how you got out," Abby says, giving Sam a knowing glance, although it wasn't entirely his fault since I was the one who left the house.

Once I am inside and get something to eat, I enter the solarium and join Wickett and Kali who are already enjoying the warm sunshine as it streams in through the large windows. As I sit with them looking outside, I think about all the things I have seen and done in my short life. I am back in my new home once again. This time, I figure I'll stay inside, at least for a while, anyway. I remember that Chester used to go outside, but he lives in a different type of environment than I do. The only types of predators in Chester's neighborhood are bullies like Carlo and Murray. And both Chester and Buster know how to deal with them. It's probably a lot safer exploring a neighborhood full of houses than exploring the middle of an unfamiliar forest. Besides, I don't want to be anybody's meal ticket.

After what seems to be a long period of self-reflection, I turn from staring out the window to tell Wickett and Kali about all the things I have seen in the woods. I tell them about the big brown dogs, the forest and its wetland, the dozens of squirrels, where I had slept for the night, my near miss with a hawk and how Toby and Inky had saved me, and my visit to the old cemetery. I don't tell them about my father, though. That's a story I think I'll save for later—perhaps when they're older and can understand better. They're still fairly young.

Thinking about the story of my walk in the woods and my visit to the pet cemetery, Kali is the first to speak. She thoughtfully looks up through the skylight into the clear blue sky and says, "I wonder who our mothers are and where they are now."

"We were just kittens when we were adopted," Wickett adds as she looks in my direction. "We only know that we came from an animal shelter—the same one you came from."

Their remarks cause me to think about the conversations I had earlier with Willow and Jenna when I was at the shelter. I don't say anything to them about my suspicions. I just smile as I look at Kali with her one ear that bends slightly forward at its very tip. Was it a matter of simple genetics or just an oddball coincidence? The prospect does exist that I may have met their mothers and, at the same time, had found my own sisters. My only regret is that I may never know what has become of my brother or my mother.

I have also left friends behind who I will never see again. I wonder where Chester, Buster, Lilly, Amos, Ollie, Olive, and Bracken are and wonder what they're doing. I miss them, but I'm grateful that they have been a part of my life. They have helped make me who I am. I know that I'll always remember them, and I'm glad to finally have a family once again.

Being homeless, I've learned that you have to take life the way it comes to you and make the best of it. Life's pathway has a lot of twists and turns to it. It has for me. I find myself reflecting on many things this afternoon, just as I had on a cold January night that seemed so long ago when I was alone and wasn't sure I'd see the next morning. I realize now, more than ever, how others affect our lives and become part of us as we age and learn from our experiences. I have grown up in so many ways. My story isn't at an end, though, only at a beginning—a new path on which my journey continues. There is no single answer to everything, just many more questions as we age.

The late afternoon sun peers over the tops of the large oak trees as it begins to find the horizon. Clouds form, casting familiar shadows across the lawn. The intermittent yet distinctive beams of sunlight from a blemished sky create a warm, glimmering glow throughout the solarium. I turn back once again to look outside and catch a single reflection of myself in one of the large windowpanes. It reminds me of the last time I saw my mother as a reflection of our two images, side by side, sitting next to that old broken hand-mirror. Only one image remains now, but there will always be two that I will remember. The memory of that day brings a tearful smile as I stare at my single reflection. My past life will always remain a part of who I am.

My story is true for all of us. During these first two years of my life, I have learned so much in so little time. It doesn't seem that long ago when I heard my mother and father call my name for the first time. I remember the journey in the forest with my father like it was only yesterday. And now I've completed that journey by following a different path—only this time by myself. It was a path that was mine alone to travel, wherever it led.

Each of us encounters obstacles during our lives, some more than others. There is uncertainty in everyone's life. Mine is no exception. I am who I am today because of both the good and bad things that have happened in my life. I guess we all have a better understanding of our lives as we age. I don't profess to know all the answers, not even as I become more aware of life as I get older. But you must persist and give life a chance to work itself out.

My name is Stimpson, and this is my third and final name. My life has come round to a full circle. I'm no longer a vagabond or alone, and the world is new once again. It is such a beautiful day...

Epilogue

Those first two years of my life account for perhaps the first sixteen to twenty years of yours. A lot of things can happen in that period of time. It did for me. I learned a lot from being on my own, as well as a lot about myself. I also learned to appreciate my life and everything and everyone who made me who I am today.

"Well, we're done," I hear Sam say. "I've finished." I'm lying on a padded mat on Sam's desk by his office window when he wakes me with those words. It's late in the afternoon, and it has started to snow—not my favorite time of year, for obvious reasons. I sit up and twirl around, diverting my attention from the window and the white drifting flakes of a new winter just in time to see that Sam has finished marking up the last pages of my story.

"How's that read? Is that okay with you?" Sam asks as he gives me a happy, slightly crooked smile and continues looking at me, wanting to connect in any way he can. "I know it's not entirely accurate because I don't know everything you went through before we brought you home from the animal shelter. But I've done my best to piece together how you came to us."

I sit, watch him, and listen to what he has to say about putting my story together. He looks directly at me, leans back in his chair, and slightly pushes away from his desk as he continues talking. "The veterinarian's report mentions that your fur had been singed in places. So I checked with a couple of fire departments in the local area. It looks like there was a fire just a few hours before that massive snowstorm you were in. The fire was contained in the basement of a tenement building, and the investigation report states that two of the firemen saw one cat drag another one out of harm's way early that same night. I talked with a few of them, and they told me they had never seen anything like it before. Did you have anything to do with that?"

I just grin at Sam's remark—a happy remembrance of a friend who had survived that night so many of my years ago.

Looking quizzically at me, Sam continues. "From what information I've managed to gather, I've tried to piece together your story as best I could. I even located that old dumpster where you were found, next to a diner. It's hard for me to imagine what you went through on your own. It sure looks like you had a rough start. I just think people should hear your story, knowing that life is an uncertainty and can be difficult for all of us."

I get up, walk to the edge of Sam's desk, and put my paw on the manuscript, giving him a knowing look. We've been together for quite a few years, almost eighteen. I'm almost twenty years old now. It's ironic that when we're young, it seems like you can't wait to grow up and be on your own. And when you get older, just the opposite occurs—you want time to slow down.

"It's not entirely fact, but you got most of it right," I meow, giving him a vibrant, insistent response, hoping he understands. I've helped him write my story on several occasions, walking on his keyboard and at times sitting directly in front of his monitor so he had to stop typing. He never shooed me off, though. I think making him pause gave him time to reflect upon what he was trying to say about my life. I confess, however, that perhaps there were a few times when I may have been a bit of a hindrance.

I think he knows I'm happy with it, because as I sit down on top of the final stack of paper, he smiles at me, gives me a long, caring pat on my head, a stroke under my chin, and puts his head down, touching mine.

Dedication

For Stimpson...

This book is dedicated to Stimpson, an abandoned cat, who brought about this story of life's possibilities and lessons from which we all can learn. Just remember—all the things that happen to us are important in making us who we are.

This book is dedicated to homeless animals like him including Mittens, Heidi, Kali, Wickett, Bentley, Jasmine, and Stormy, all who were abandoned and have shared their lives with my wife and me. It is for all those people who have the compassion to adopt these animals, provide for them, and give them a loving home, and for all the animal shelters and the volunteers who help these orphans. This story is also for my sister Maribeth, who operates 'God's Little Critters,' a shelter for the care and rehabilitation of injured and orphaned wild animals. And for my sister Debbie, who loved her four cats, and sadly passed away the day after I completed the final version of the manuscript, not ever having a chance to read it.

And it is for you, the reader. I can only hope that you might understand and learn from it—to pause and reflect. Never forget that these animals teach us compassion, trust, and love throughout the years, and so much more about ourselves. Important people in our lives pass away, and so do the animals that have become a part of our family. It perhaps can be difficult in some ways to let go, because they can never talk to you, at least not with words. You can only hope they understand how you feel about them. All of them have their own life stories to tell. Like people, they have a story we can all share. This is one of those stories.

Portions of this story are true. Other portions are only what I could have imagined Stimpson's life was like in that first winter, alone. He found a new home when my wife noticed his picture in that old newsletter so many years ago and picked him up at an animal shelter in Kennebunk, Maine. He lived for almost 18 years with us until he `was about twenty. And then he became very ill on my birthday and died early in the morning on the following day. I think about him often as I write and miss him every day. He was such a help to me. He still is. I miss those big green eyes of his and the way he always looked up at me when I spoke to him, and those many times when we looked out the window at the world together, wondering what the next day would bring...

About the Author

Russell H. Plante is an Engineering Physicist with a diverse engineering and academic background in Engineering Physics, Electrical Engineering, and Business Administration. A skilled technical writer, he is a previously published author with John Wiley & Sons, Inc. and Academic Press (Elsevier) and continues to write in both non-fiction and fiction genres. He resides with his wife Kathy and their three cats in Kittery, Maine where there's always a chance of a blizzard and some time to write meaningful stories during a long cold winter.

www.ingramcontent.com/pod-product-compliance
Lightning Source LLC
Chambersburg PA
CBHW021058130626
46552CB00005B/2156